# Diseases and Disorders

# Birth Defects

## by Barbara Sheen

**LUCENT BOOKS**
*An imprint of Thomson Gale, a part of The Thomson Corporation*

**THOMSON**
TM
**GALE**

Detroit • New York • San Francisco • San Diego • New Haven, Conn.
Waterville, Maine • London • Munich

**LIBRARY OF CONGRESS CATALOGING-IN-PUBLICATION DATA**

Sheen, Barbara.
   Birth defects / by Barbara Sheen.
     p. cm. — (Diseases and disorders)
   Includes bibliographical references and index.
   Contents: What are birth defects?—Diagnosing and treating birth defects—Living with birth defects—Preventing birth defects—What the future holds.
   ISBN 1-59018-406-8 (hard cover : alk. paper)
   1. Abnormalities, Human—Juvenile literature. 2. Fetus—Abnormalities—Juvenile literature. 3. Genetic disorders—Juvenile literature. I. Title. II. Diseases and disorders series.
   RG626.S54 2005
   618.3'2—dc22

                                                 2004022547

Printed in the United States of America

# *Table of Contents*

# "The Most Difficult Puzzles Ever Devised"

CHARLES BEST, ONE of the pioneers in the search for a cure for diabetes, once explained what it is about medical research that intrigued him so. "It's not just the gratification of knowing one is helping people," he confided, "although that probably is a more heroic and selfless motivation. Those feelings may enter in, but truly, what I find best is the feeling of going toe to toe with nature, of trying to solve the most difficult puzzles ever devised. The answers are there somewhere, those keys that will solve the puzzle and make the patient well. But how will those keys be found?"

Since the dawn of civilization, nothing has so puzzled people—and often frightened them, as well—as the onset of illness in a body or mind that had seemed healthy before. A seizure, the inability of a heart to pump, the sudden deterioration of muscle tone in a small child—being unable to reverse such conditions or even to understand why they occur was unspeakably frustrating to healers. Even before there were names for such conditions, even before they were understood at all, each was a reminder of how complex the human body was, and how vulnerable.

While our grappling with understanding diseases has been frustrating at times, it has also provided some of humankind's most heroic accomplishments. Alexander Fleming's accidental discovery in 1928 of a mold that could be turned into penicillin has resulted in the saving of untold millions of lives. The isolation of the enzyme insulin has reversed what was once a death sentence for anyone with diabetes. There have been great strides in combating conditions for which there are not yet cures, too. Medicines can help AIDS patients live longer, diagnostic tools such as mammography and ultrasounds can help doctors find tumors while they are treatable, and laser surgery techniques have made the most intricate, minute operations routine.

This "toe-to-toe" competition with diseases and disorders is even more remarkable when seen in a historical continuum. An astonishing amount of progress has been made in a very short time. Just two hundred years ago, the existence of germs as a cause of some diseases was unknown. In fact, it was less than 150 years ago that a British surgeon named Joseph Lister had difficulty persuading his fellow doctors that washing their hands before delivering a baby might increase the chances of a healthy delivery (especially if they had just attended to a diseased patient)!

Each book in Lucent's Diseases and Disorders series explores a disease or disorder and the knowledge that has been accumulated (or discarded) by doctors through the years. Each book also examines the tools used for pinpointing a diagnosis, as well as the various means that are used to treat or cure a disease. Finally, new ideas are presented—techniques or medicines that may be on the horizon.

Frustration and disappointment are still part of medicine, for not every disease or condition can be cured or prevented. But the limitations of knowledge are being pushed outward constantly; the "most difficult puzzles ever devised" are finding challengers every day.

# A Common Problem

I F A GROUP OF people with birth defects were gathered together, it would be hard for an outsider to determine what the participants have in common. This is because they and the challenges they face are so diverse. Among the group are males and females of every ethnicity. Their ages range from newborn to the elderly. Some members of the group show no visible signs of illness, but a birth defect has affected the way their hearts, lungs, kidneys, brains, or other internal organs function. Some have visible problems such as missing and malformed body parts. Others cannot walk without assistance. Some cannot speak, or use their hands, while still others have hearing loss and visual impairments. This is because birth defects can affect any organ in the body. And, the size of this group of people is extremely large. Every three and a half minutes a baby in the United States is born with a birth defect, which means that 150,000 babies with birth defects are born in the United States each year. That number equals one out of every twenty-eight babies.

Spencer was one of those babies. He was born four months early with defects in his lungs, eyes, circulation, and brain. As a result, he spent the first four months of his life in the hospital where he endured four different types of surgeries. His father recalls: "You think the day your first child is born is going to be a wonderful day, but for us it was a terrifying day. It was a lot to go through."[1]

Fortunately, Spencer's problems were correctable. Today he is a healthy two-year-old. His mother explains: "Looking at him

6

now—he is just perfect and beautiful. We have an incredible little man who is just a joy."[2]

## Changed Lives

Unfortunately, not all birth defects can be corrected. Some are fatal. Indeed, 20 percent of all infant deaths in the United States are linked to certain birth defects. Other birth defects cause long-term disabilities that affect an individual throughout his or her lifetime. Fifteen-year-old Jimmy, for example, was born with spina bifida, a crippling birth defect. As a consequence, Jimmy's life is much different than if he had been born healthy. Jimmy has had to undergo at least fifteen different surgeries, and he is confined to a wheelchair.

*Many children with birth defects show no visible signs of illness. This young girl, for example, was born with a blood disorder.*

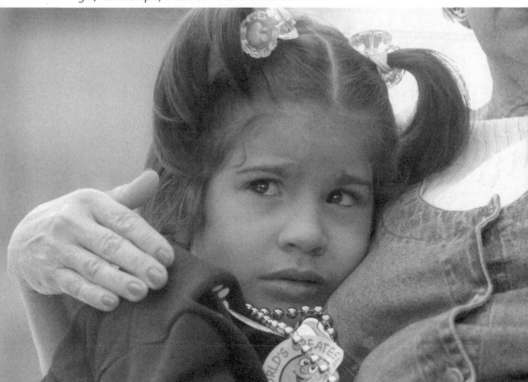

## The Impact on Others

The family members of individuals with birth defects face challenges as well. Many people with birth defects must be cared for all their lives. Often it is their parents and siblings who must assume this responsibility. This can be both an emotional and financial burden for families and society. Indeed, a 2003 study conducted by researchers at Research Triangle International in North Carolina and the Centers for Disease Control estimates the financial cost of four different birth defects: mental retardation, cerebral palsy, hearing loss, and vision impairment. Including the medical costs, cost of special equipment and special education, and loss of workplace productivity, the estimated average lifetime cost per person ranges from $417,000 for individuals with hearing loss to more than $1 million for individuals with mental retardation.

## Misunderstandings

Making matters worse, many parents of children with birth defects feel guilty. They wonder if something they did caused their child's problem. The mother of a child with Down syndrome, a birth defect that causes mental disabilities, recalls: "I gave birth to my daughter Katie, who was immediately diagnosed with Down syndrome. I was devastated and in shock. I was a young, healthy woman and tried to think back what I had done wrong during my pregnancy that could have caused this."[3]

## Importance of Education

Katie's mother did not do anything wrong. But because she did not know much about birth defects, she was left wondering. She is not alone. Many other individuals know little about birth defects. But, unlike Katie's mother, their lack of knowledge can allow them to make unhealthy choices that negatively impact their

*Born with spina bifida, this wheelchair-bound boy is the March of Dimes ambassador to his Oklahoma middle school, where he is also a cheerleader.*

baby. Many birth defects can be prevented when women know what behaviors to avoid. That is why it is so important that people learn all they can about birth defects. By knowing what causes birth defects, individuals can make decisions that will help protect their baby and prevent many birth defects. Missy, an expectant mother, explains: "I am going to have my first baby and I don't know if I have made the right decisions during the first three months. It is important to educate mothers before they get pregnant."[4]

Because learning about birth defects is so important, organizations such as the March of Dimes, which is dedicated to preventing birth defects, and the U.S. Congress are working together to educate the American public. In fact, in 2002 Congress passed the Birth Defect Prevention Act, which has as one of its goals informing and educating the public about birth defects. An expert at the March of Dimes explains: "It is critical that women and their health care providers be educated about what they can do to improve birth outcomes."[5]

## Knowledge Is Power

Learning about specific birth defects can also help individuals with birth defects and their loved ones make informed decisions concerning their health. It can help them to understand the challenges they face and give them tools to help them cope. Ingrid, who has lived for almost forty years with a debilitating birth defect called sickle-cell anemia, explains:

> The doctors did not expect me to live past my sixth birthday. . . .
> Despite the bleak outlook and shortened life expectancy predicted by the doctors . . . I am here to tell my story almost four decades later. I have been blessed with a supportive family. . . .
> Their efforts included making sure they learned as much as they could about the disease and then passing that knowledge on to me so that I could, in turn, take care of myself. . . . Knowledge is indeed power.[6]

# Chapter 1

# What Are Birth Defects?

**B**IRTH DEFECTS ARE abnormalities of the structure or function of the body. Birth defects occur as a result of problems in a fetus's development. Faulty genes, inherited diseases, and outside or unknown factors cause such problems. The resulting birth defects, of which there are more than five thousand different types, can be serious or minor.

## Physical Effects of Birth Defects

All birth defects have a physical effect on a person, which varies significantly depending on the specific birth defect. Structural birth defects affect the physical makeup of the body. When a baby has a structural birth defect, some part of the body is missing or malformed. The affected body part can be internal or external. Structural birth defects such as a missing or extra finger or toe can be relatively harmless, but the absence of kidneys or lack of development of parts of the brain can be fatal. Some structural birth defects, such as a clubfoot, affect an individual's ability to walk. Cleft palates impair speech, while malformed or missing fingers or hands affect a person's fine motor skills. Gastrointestinal defects, which involve incomplete development of the esophagus, stomach, intestines, or rectum, lead to problems swallowing and digesting food and eliminating waste.

Functional birth defects affect the way the body works. Depending on the organs involved, functional birth defects can cause problems throughout the body. For example, problems in the functioning of the brain cause learning disabilities, mental

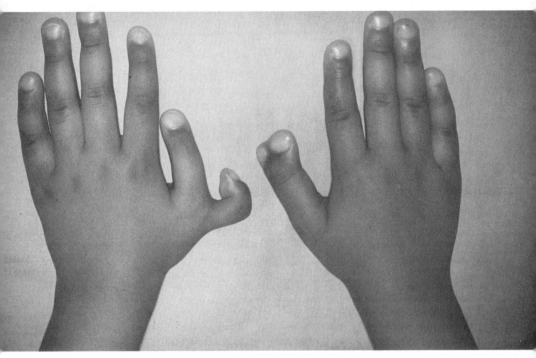

*Being born with extra fingers, like the child in this photo, is an example of a structural birth defect.*

retardation, deafness, blindness, speech problems, and limited mobility. Other functional birth defects can affect a person's circulation, breathing, and digestion. Inherited diseases are functional birth defects.

Functional birth defects can cause secondary problems. For instance, many people with cerebral palsy, a birth defect that affects the part of the brain that controls movement, often have seizures. Problems in the development of their brains cause normal electrical connections to be disrupted. Secondary problems are also common with structural defects like spina bifida, where underdeveloped nerves lead to paralysis, lack of bowel and bladder control, brain malformations, and learning disabilities.

Compromised respiratory and circulatory systems in two other birth defects, cystic fibrosis and sickle-cell anemia, cause weakness and fatigue and make individuals susceptible to infections.

When the body's cells receive insufficient oxygen due to sickle-cell anemia, individuals experience episodes of intense pain. Heidy, a young woman with sickle-cell anemia, explains: "I've been hospitalized over 100 times for pain episodes. . . . Sometimes the pain was ok, sometimes I felt as if I were about to die."[7]

## Genes, the Body's Instruction Manual

Birth defects have many different causes. Often the culprit is a faulty gene. Genes are the body's instruction manual. They are contained in forty-six capsulelike structures called chromosomes, which are found in every cell in the body.

Chromosomes are organized into twenty-three pairs. Each pair of chromosomes contains 140,000 genes that give a person his or her unique characteristics and tell the body how to develop and function.

When a fetus is conceived, each parent passes on twenty-three chromosomes containing seventy thousand genes. The chromosomes pair up within the fertilized egg, which divides and redivides, forming new cells. Each new cell contains two copies of the original seventy thousand genes. Each time a fetus is conceived, each parent passes on one-half of each pair of genes, but in different combinations. The result is that every person, with the exception of identical twins, receives a different mix of genes. This is why siblings do not always look alike.

Occasionally a defective gene is passed on in the mix. The damaged gene gives developing cells faulty instructions. As a consequence, the organs and body parts formed with the affected cells develop abnormally. Sometimes they do not develop at all.

Birth defects such as missing fingers, hearing loss, and visual problems are often caused in this manner. So too are malformed internal organs such as kidneys, lungs, brains, and hearts. Indeed, heart defects are the most common birth defect. Eighty-seven babies are born with a heart defect every day, compared to twenty-seven a day born with cerebral palsy or sickle-cell anemia. David was born with a heart defect. A report on his birth reads: "David Rose, only minutes old was fighting for his life. His tiny heart wasn't pumping enough oxygen-rich red blood

# Fetal Development

Over the nine months that a woman is pregnant, the fetus goes through many stages of development. If all goes well during each stage of development the baby is normal and healthy. When something goes wrong, a birth defect can develop.

When the sperm and egg first unite, cells start dividing to form an embryo. In the first month of pregnancy the embryo grows to be about half an inch long. Brain cells begin to develop, as do arms and legs. The eyes also form, although scientists doubt the embryo can see.

In the next two months internal organs begin to develop, as do fingers and other body parts. The embryo reaches three to four inches in length, and is now known as a fetus. Brain cells continue to grow, and by the end of the third month the fetus's heart is pumping blood. His or her sexual organs are also formed. At this time the fetus's gender can be determined.

During the second three months of pregnancy the fetus grows to about a foot in length and about one and one-half pounds in weight. By this time the fetus can open and close its eyes and move its fingers. The mother can feel the fetus moving inside her. By the sixth month, the fetus has hair. Despite all this growth, many of the fetus's organs, such as the lungs and brain, are not yet fully developed.

In the last three months of pregnancy the fetus starts making body fat and gaining weight. During this time brain growth continues.

Once all the organs have fully developed and the baby is large enough to survive on its own, the baby is born. This usually occurs after forty weeks of pregnancy.

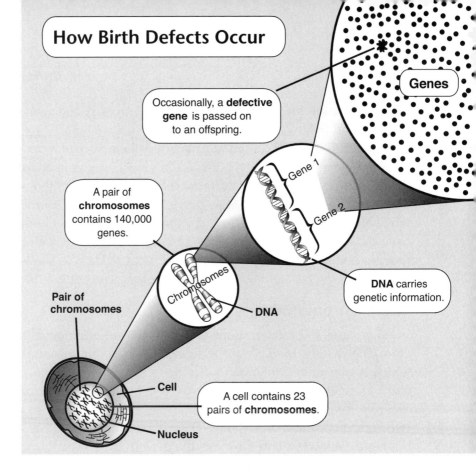

**How Birth Defects Occur**

Occasionally, a **defective gene** is passed on to an offspring.

Genes

A pair of **chromosomes** contains 140,000 genes.

Gene 1

Gene 2

Pair of chromosomes

Chromosomes

**DNA** carries genetic information.

DNA

Cell

A cell contains 23 pairs of **chromosomes**.

Nucleus

throughout his body. . . . [He was] diagnosed with . . . a complex of four heart defects that kept some of his blood from circulating to his lungs and picking up the oxygen he needed to survive."[8]

## Inherited Diseases

Inherited diseases are also transmitted through genes. If there is a family history of an inherited disease, a gene that causes the disease can be passed to the fetus from either parent. Moreover, parents can carry and pass on a disease gene even if they are unaffected by the disease. Once the gene is transmitted, the baby may develop the disease or, like the parent, become a carrier.

Whether or not the baby develops the disease depends on a number of factors. In some cases both parents must transmit the defective gene in order for the disease to develop. This is the case in cystic fibrosis, an inherited disease that affects the breathing and digestion of one out of every thirty-three hundred babies born in the United States each year. Also caused in this fashion are Tay-Sachs disease, a fatal disorder of the nervous system; thalassemia; and sickle-cell anemia.

Thalassemia and sickle-cell anemia affect the ability of a person's red blood cells to deliver oxygen and nutrition to the body. Of the two, sickle-cell anemia is more common. Over sixty thousand Americans have the disease. Derrick and Laquana, a couple who both carry the sickle-cell gene, explain: "Turns out we both have the sickle trait. . . . We know it won't be easy, but we've thought about it a lot. If the baby is born with sickle cell, she is going to get the best loving and caring any baby can get."[9]

## The X Chromosome

In other cases the mother alone can transmit an inherited disease. The disease is likely to be linked to an X chromosome, which is transmitted by a mother to her fetus. A male has only one X chromosome, which he receives from his mother, and one Y chromosome, which he receives from his father. A female has two X chromosomes, one from each parent. If a male fetus does not have a normal X chromosome, the defective X chromosome directs his body to develop the inherited disease. For example, if a mother carries a faulty X chromosome that causes color blindness, a disorder in which certain colors cannot be distinguished, her daughters will not inherit the disease because each will have another X chromosome that is not linked to color blindness. Her sons will inherit it because each will have only the faulty X chromosome.

## Dominant Genes

Other inherited disorders can be transmitted to male or female babies from either the mother or the father. This occurs when the problematic gene is a dominant gene. Some genes are dominant while others are recessive. When a dominant gene is present for a certain trait, whether or not it is a defective gene, the baby always inherits that trait. Recessive traits, on the other hand, are only inherited if no dominant genes are present. For example, genes for brown eyes are dominant. Therefore, if a fetus inherits one brown-eye gene and one blue-eye gene, the baby will have

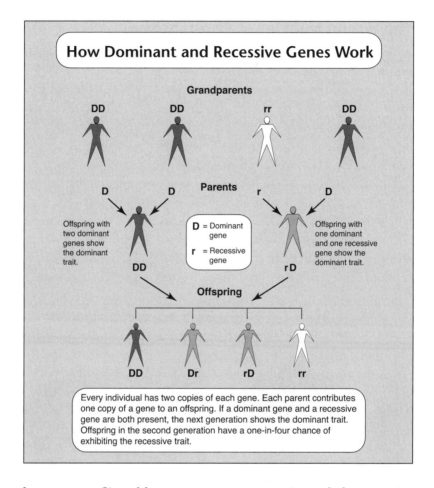

**How Dominant and Recessive Genes Work**

**Grandparents**

DD   DD   rr   DD

D   D   **Parents**   r   D

Offspring with two dominant genes show the dominant trait.

D = Dominant gene

r = Recessive gene

DD

rD

Offspring with one dominant and one recessive gene show the dominant trait.

**Offspring**

DD   Dr   rD   rr

Every individual has two copies of each gene. Each parent contributes one copy of a gene to an offspring. If a dominant gene and a recessive gene are both present, the next generation shows the dominant trait. Offspring in the second generation have a one-in-four chance of exhibiting the recessive trait.

brown eyes. Since blue-eye genes are recessive, a baby must inherit a pair of blue-eye genes in order to have blue eyes.

Muscular dystrophy, a disease characterized by progressive muscle weakness, and fragile X syndrome, a disorder characterized by mental impairment, are caused by dominant mutant genes. When a disease is passed to the fetus in this manner, the parent may have the disease or be a carrier. David, a man with fragile X syndrome, explains: "I have fragile X syndrome and so do both of my daughters. I am 40 years old and from a very early age, I knew I was 'different' from others. . . . Now I am married . . . I have three children, two girls and a 3 year old boy. Both of my daughters have fragile X."[10]

## The Wrong Number of Chromosomes

Birth defects also develop when a fetus inherits twenty-four rather than twenty-three chromosomes from either parent. When this happens the fertilized egg contains forty-seven instead of forty-six chromosomes. As the egg divides, cells form with an extra chromosome. Genes in the extra chromosome alter normal fetal development by giving the developing body instructions it cannot follow. The result is a disorder called Down syndrome.

Down syndrome is characterized by developmental disabilities such as mental retardation, as well as physical impairments. Jim, whose son Kevin has Down syndrome, explains: "Whereas most people have forty-six chromosomes, Kevin has forty-seven. He has an extra twenty-first chromosome. . . . This problem occurs at conception, during the initial cell division, and it is totally random."[11]

*The boy at the top center of this photo has Down syndrome, a birth defect caused by having too many chromosomes.*

## Outside Factors

Even when there are no genetic abnormalities, birth defects often develop when the fetus is exposed to potentially harmful substances. Any substance that enters a pregnant woman's bloodstream is transmitted to the developing fetus through the placenta. Consequently, the fetus is exposed to everything that enters the mother's blood, whether by mouth, air, or intravenously. So, if an expectant mother uses cocaine, for example, the fetus is exposed to the harmful effects of the drug.

Substances like alcohol, cigarettes, medications, illegal drugs, contaminated food, household chemicals, and infectious agents all can lead to birth defects. This is because fetal cells are undeveloped and fragile, so the fetus is more sensitive and vulnerable to the effects of these substances. Some substances do not harm the mother, but they damage the fetus. When the substance can hurt the mother, it has an even more pronounced effect on the fetus. The damage can take place any time during pregnancy, but the fetus is most vulnerable in the first trimester, when brain cells are developing.

For example, alcohol can have a harmful effect on anyone, especially when it is abused. Small quantities of alcohol, such as an occasional glass of wine, usually do not harm an adult but have the potential to cause fetal alcohol syndrome (FAS), a birth disorder caused when the fetus is exposed to alcohol. Such exposure can cause mental retardation, hearing and vision problems, growth deficiencies, and facial abnormalities. As a consequence, babies born with fetal alcohol syndrome face both physical and mental disabilities.

Approximately thirty-three out of every one thousand babies born in the United States each year have fetal alcohol syndrome. Teresa, the adoptive mother of John, a young man with fetal alcohol syndrome, explains: "John has Fetal Alcohol Syndrome, a disorder caused by prenatal exposure to alcohol that has sentenced John to a life-long hangover. His birth mother's drinking during pregnancy caused John's mild retardation, small stature, unusual facial features, and damage to his central nervous system."[12]

*These three adopted brothers have fetal alcohol syndrome, a birth defect caused by their mother's abuse of alcohol during pregnancy.*

Exposure to cigarettes and illegal drugs has a similar effect on a developing fetus. Cigarette smoke has been linked to premature birth and problems in babies' lungs. Usually premature babies are extremely small and their organs are not fully developed. Therefore, they often face serious health problems at birth as well as lasting disabilities like hearing loss, blindness, heart problems, mental retardation, and cerebral palsy. Drugs like cocaine, crack, and heroin can cause bleeding in a fetus's brain. This leads to brain damage and developmental delays, including mental retardation.

Prescription drugs, too, can harm a fetus. For example, isotretinoin, a drug used to treat acne and commonly called Accutane, works by slowing the growth of skin cells in individuals with acne. The drug is so powerful, however, that when a fetus is exposed to it, isotretinoin slows or stops the growth of all fetal cells. As a consequence, 35 percent of all babies born to pregnant women treated with the drug are born with birth defects. These include blindness, mental retardation, malformed organs, and physical deformities. Because of the danger isotretinoin presents to unborn babies, the Food and Drug Administration warns women: "You must not become pregnant while taking Accutane. . . . There is an extremely high risk that your baby will be deformed or will die if you are pregnant while taking Accutane."[13]

Household chemicals like those used in paints, cleaning solvents, and pesticides have a similar effect. Although exposure to low levels of most chemicals poses little risk, daily heavy exposure, such as that which pregnant women in the dry cleaning or house painting business experience, can interfere with the formation and growth of fetal nerve cells. This can cause learning disabilities and mental retardation in the baby.

## Infectious Agents

Since a fetus has an undeveloped immune system, it cannot fight off the damaging effects of infectious agents. This makes fetuses especially vulnerable to infection. For example, the virus that causes *Rubella* or German measles does not usually cause serious problems in individuals with a functioning immune system, but

*This baby's cloudy pupils reveal the cataracts she was born with because her mother had* Rubella *(German measles) early in her pregnancy.*

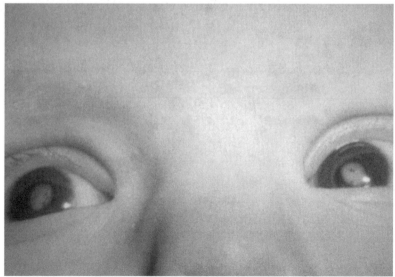

it causes a variety of birth defects in a fetus. Deafness, vision problems, heart defects, and cerebral palsy are all linked to fetal exposure to the rubella virus.

Infectious agents that cause sexually transmitted diseases can also cause birth defects when a baby is exposed to the infectious agents as the baby passes through the birth canal. Exposure to these germs can cause blindness, hearing loss, cerebral palsy, and mental retardation.

Other infectious agents such as *Listeria*, a bacterium that causes food poisoning, also affect fetal brain development. *Listeria* is such a threat to the welfare of unborn babies that in 1992 the Centers for Disease Control issued a warning advising pregnant women to avoid eating processed meats such as bologna, which is sometimes tainted with *Listeria*. Pregnant women exposed to listeria do get sick, but it is the fetus who is most in danger.

# Infections and Birth Defects

*Listeria* and *Rubella* are not the only infectious agents that cause birth defects. Others include the infectious agents that cause toxoplasmosis, fifth disease, chicken pox, and hepatitis B.

Toxoplasmosis is an infection that is transmitted through cat feces. If a pregnant woman is infected with toxoplasmosis, it can cause learning disabilities, eye infections, an enlarged liver, mental retardation, and cerebral palsy to develop in the fetus. Fifth disease is a flulike virus, known to cause heart problems in babies.

In some cases exposure to an infectious agent not only causes birth defects but causes the baby to be born with the disease. This occurs in hepatitis B and chicken pox. For example, a fetus exposed to the virus that causes chicken pox may be born with a severe case of

## Poor Nutrition

When a pregnant woman fails to eat enough vital nutrients, birth defects can also develop. Good nutrition during pregnancy helps a fetus to grow and develop normally. Calcium is needed for bones to grow. Brain cells cannot develop correctly without adequate protein. Nerve cells need folic acid, a B vitamin, to develop normally. Indeed, lack of folic acid is linked to spina bifida, a birth defect in which the neural tube that connects the brain to the spinal cord does not develop properly. As a result, the spinal cord is exposed and nerves that go from the spinal cord to the legs, bowels, and bladder do not function normally.

## Unknown Factors

Sometimes babies are born with birth defects for unknown reasons. According to the March of Dimes, the cause of 60 percent of

chicken pox and have malformed and paralyzed limbs, defective muscles and bones, a smaller than normal head, mental retardation, and blindness.

Some birth defects are the result of fetal exposure to infectious agents that cause sexually transmitted diseases. During birth, such exposure can occur in the birth canal. Exposure to genital warts in this manner can cause warts to grow on the baby's vocal cords, causing the baby to have problems making sounds. Exposure to genital herpes can cause the baby to have skin and mouth sores, brain damage, mental retardation, and blindness.

Other sexually transmitted diseases also cause damage. Syphilis can cause brain damage, cerebral palsy, blindness, and hearing loss, as well as death. Chlamydia, which is one of the most common of all sexually transmitted diseases, causes a blinding eye infection, while gonorrhea can cause a life-threatening blood infection, as well as problems in a baby's joints.

all birth defects is unknown. The most common theory is that a combination of factors is at fault, causing what scientists call multifactorial birth defects. For example, healthy genes may interact with each other and with seemingly harmless outside factors such as a dose of medicine for a cold. For unknown reasons the combination causes the genes to mutate, resulting in a birth defect. Or limited exposure to a number of outside factors may combine to cause a birth defect. For instance, a pregnant woman may be exposed to small amounts of paint solvent while painting the nursery and eat less vitamin B than is advisable. The result may be a birth defect. These combinations may cause birth defects to develop in one fetus but not another. This is because each individual responds differently to different substances. Scientists are unsure why this is so.

There are many birth defects that are believed to have unknown multifactorial causes. A clubfoot, in which the joints, bones, and muscles in the foot and ankle malform, and a cleft lip or palate, in which the mouth or lip malforms, are two examples.

## People at Risk

Birth defects can occur in any baby. However, some babies are at greater risk. These include babies born to women exposed to dangerous substances and infections, babies that do not receive adequate prenatal nutrition, and babies born to families with a history of inherited diseases.

Even when a family does not have a history of an inherited disease, members of certain ethnic groups are more likely to carry the gene for a particular inherited disease than members of other groups. For example, people of African descent are at a greater risk of developing sickle-cell anemia than individuals of other ethnicities. An estimated 1 in every 375 African Americans has the disease compared to 1 in every 72,000 Non-African Americans. And about 8 percent or 3.5 million African Americans are carriers of the sickle-cell gene.

Cystic fibrosis commonly affects Caucasians of northern European descent. About 1 in 22 Americans of northern European descent carries the gene, and 1 in every 1,600 Caucasians is born with the disease. This compares to 1 in every 13,000 African Americans, and 1 in every 50,000 Asians.

In a like manner, Jews of eastern European descent are at greater risk of Tay-Sachs disease. An estimated 1 in 27 Jews of eastern European descent are carriers, while only 1 in 250 Jews not of eastern European descent carry the gene. A Jewish woman explains: "When I was pregnant, we were warned that the baby could have Tay-Sachs disease because we're Jewish and some of our family are of Eastern European descent. Fortunately, the baby was fine. We were lucky."[14]

## Mother's Age

A pregnant woman's age can also put a baby at risk. Babies with Down syndrome are more likely to be born to older mothers. According to the March of Dimes, the chance of a woman in her twenties having a baby with Down syndrome is 1 in 1,230. At age thirty-five the chance is 1 in 270. At forty the risk rises to 1 in 78, and at forty-five the chance increases to 1 in 22. Scientists do not know why this is so.

Other problems arise because older mothers are likely to give birth to more than one baby per pregnancy. This is often because many older women have difficulties becoming pregnant and use fertility treatments, which encourage multiple gestations.

For a woman of any age, multiple births put a baby at risk of birth defects. One reason is that multiple fetuses must share nutrients, oxygen, and blood. Therefore, they receive less of these vital substances than a single fetus. It is not surprising then that almost 60 percent of twins, 90 percent of triplets, and almost all higher multiple births are born prematurely, putting them at risk of developing cerebral palsy and other birth defects linked to premature births.

Identical twins face an extra risk. Because identical twins form from one egg that divides and forms two fetuses, only one placenta connects both of them to the mother. Fifteen percent of identical twins develop a problem called twin-to-twin transfusion syndrome, in which the shared placenta contains abnormal blood vessels that send too much blood to one fetus and not enough to the other. If not corrected through surgery, both babies can die.

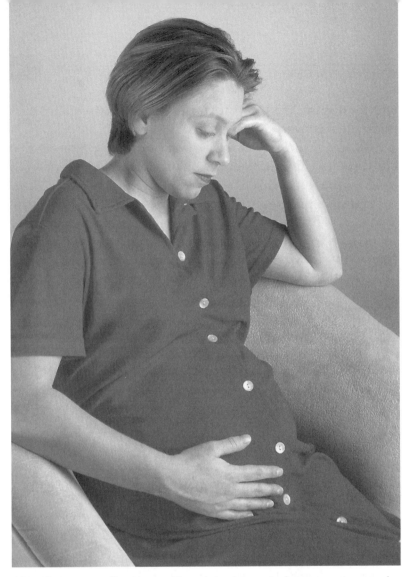

*Many factors can affect the health and development of a pregnant woman's fetus, including viruses, environmental poisons, and even her age.*

## Obesity

Obesity also raises the risk of birth defects. Obese and overweight women have an increased risk of having babies with heart abnormalities, spina bifida, and omphalocele, a defect in which the baby's intestines protrude through the navel. According to the Centers for Disease Control, 9 to 15 percent of babies born to obese women have a serious birth defect compared to 3 to 5 percent of babies born to women of normal weight. Centers for Disease Control epidemiologist Margaret Watkins explains: "This is yet another adverse health outcome associated with overweight and obesity and people need to know that."[15]

Scientists have not determined why obesity raises the risk of birth defects. They theorize that many obese women have poor eating habits. They often consume nutrient-poor junk food rather than more nourishing foods. This may lead to the fetus not getting adequate protein, calcium, and B vitamins.

Clearly, with so many different types of birth defects there is also a wide array of causes and risk factors. No matter the cause, birth defects have a physical impact on individuals' bodies and on their lives.

# Chapter 2

# Diagnosing and Treating Birth Defects

S INCE THERE ARE so many different types of birth defects, both diagnosis and treatment depend on the specific problem. In some cases diagnostic tests administered to pregnant women can detect birth defects in the fetus. Other birth defects are identified at birth, while some birth defects are not recognizable for months or years.

No matter when a birth defect is detected, with appropriate treatment many birth defects can be corrected. When this is not possible, treatment can relieve the symptoms of incurable birth defects.

## Blood Tests

About 250 birth defects can be identified before a baby is born, including Down syndrome, spina bifida, heart defects, gastrointestinal and kidney malformations, and missing and malformed limbs. Tests administered to expectant mothers detect these problems.

When a pregnant woman first visits a doctor, she is given a blood test. The test determines the mother's blood type and whether she does or does not have a protein in her blood known as the Rh factor. There is no problem if the mother's blood contains this protein. If her blood does not, however, but the father's blood does, the fetus's blood will also contain it. This makes the mother's and the fetus's blood incompatible. When this occurs, the mother's immune system produces antibodies that attack the fetus, causing cerebral palsy and heart problems. To prevent this, a series of injections are given to the mother. These prevent the production of the destructive antibodies.

Another blood test is administered between the sixteenth and eighteenth week of pregnancy. Known as a triple-marker test, it measures the levels of a protein, alpha-fetoprotein, produced by the fetus, as well as two hormones that pregnant women manufacture. Although these substances are found in all pregnant women's blood, abnormally high levels indicate, but do not guarantee, that the fetus is affected with Down syndrome or spina bifida.

## Ultrasound

An ultrasound test is administered in the same time frame as the triple-marker test. It allows the doctor to see how the fetus is developing and how fetal organs are forming and functioning. Structural defects are often, but not always, detected with ultrasound.

*A woman receives an ultrasound test during her pregnancy. Ultrasounds help doctors to detect birth defects early in pregnancy.*

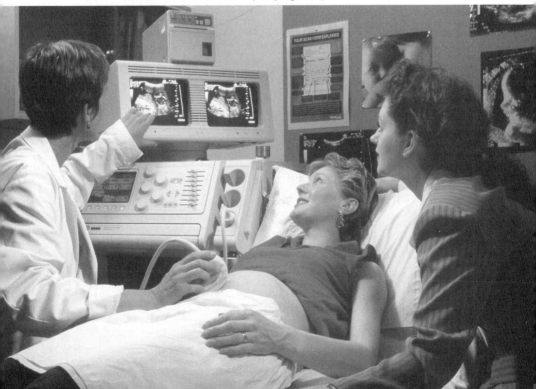

During an ultrasound test the health care professional rubs a special sound-conducting gel on the pregnant woman's abdomen. Then, a small handheld device similar to a scanning wand is passed across the pregnant woman's internal organs. It produces sound waves that bounce off the woman's abdomen back to the wand. The reflected sound waves form a pattern, which a computer program translates into an image of the fetus on a computer monitor. Author Mitchell Zuckoff describes expectant parents Tierney and Greg's experience:

> Kolano [the health care professional] moved the ultrasound wand over Tierney's jelly-covered skin like a pizza maker using a ladle to spread sauce on a mound of dough. With each movement of the wand, Kolano created a picture of the tiny creature inside. Greg studied the monitor, fascinated by the details emerging from what looked like a half-developed Polaroid. An arm here, a leg there, a tiny profile. Then the internal organs: brain, liver, kidneys.[16]

If there are any abnormalities, they usually show up when the ultrasound is passed over the affected part of the fetus. An ultrasound test diagnosed a kidney defect in Cindy's niece. She explains: "An ultrasound that was done long before the baby was born found a hole in the baby's kidneys. The doctor said it would affect her ability to urinate. We all knew about it months before the baby was born and were able to prepare for it. I find that amazing."[17]

## Amniocentesis

When a pregnant woman is at risk of having a baby with a birth defect, or if other tests yield suspicious results, another test known as an amniocentesis is administered in the sixteenth to eighteenth week of pregnancy. During an amniocentesis a long thin needle is inserted through the woman's abdomen, and one ounce of amniotic fluid (the fluid that surrounds the fetus in the womb) is removed. This is typically done at the same time as an ultrasound so that the doctor can see where to place the needle without harming the fetus.

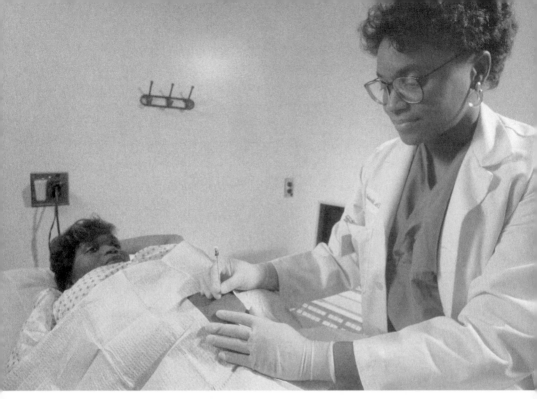

*A doctor performs an amniocentesis, in which she withdraws the fluid around her pregnant patient's fetus. The fluid will be tested for signs of Down syndrome, cystic fibrosis, and Tay-Sachs disease.*

Amniotic fluid contains fetal cells, which are analyzed in a laboratory for chromosomal and genetic abnormalities. This makes it possible to accurately diagnose Down syndrome, cystic fibrosis, and Tay-Sachs disease.

Once an amniocentesis is administered, it takes at least two weeks for the results to be established. Bonnie recalls: "They take a needle and stick it in you. The needle is so long that I thought I would faint if I looked at it. But it didn't hurt. I just felt some pressure. I didn't think they'd find any problems, but I was still very nervous until I got the results."[18]

## Diagnosis at Birth

Some birth defects are not detected until the baby is born. Because of the position of the baby in the womb, some structural birth defects such as spina bifida and malformed or missing body parts are obvious at birth but are not always detected by ultrasound. For example, Cathy's son, Jimmy, was diagnosed with

# Virginia Apgar

The Apgar test was developed by physician Virginia Apgar to ensure that newborn infants receive immediate care. Apgar's contributions to newborn health, however, reach beyond the Apgar test.

Virginia Apgar was born in 1909. Even as a child she wanted to become a doctor, though at this time few women went to college, and even fewer became doctors. But Virginia was a determined person. In 1933 she graduated from Mount Holyoke College and went on to medical school at Columbia University, where she received her medical degree.

At first she was a surgeon. But her greatest interest was in treating infants and doing whatever she could to prevent or minimize birth defects. She believed newborn babies deserved the same quality of health care as children and adults, and that identifying birth defects early would help improve a baby's chances to live a normal life. With that in mind, she developed the Apgar score.

As a result of her interest in birth defects, in 1950 she became the head of the birth defects division of the March of Dimes. In this position she traveled throughout the world making people aware of the dangers of birth defects while raising money to fund research to treat and cure them. According to an article on the Apgar.net Web site, "Virginia Apgar probably did more than any other physician to bring the problem of birth defects out of the back rooms."

She died in 1974. Twenty years later in 1994, the U.S. Postal Service issued a twenty-cent Virginia Apgar commemorative stamp to honor this great woman.

spina bifida in the delivery room. She remembers: "At birth, he had a sac (it almost looked like an inflated balloon) on his lower back. His spinal cord and nerves were exposed and damaged at this site in the lumbar region of his spine."[19]

Other less obvious birth defects are often detected immediately after birth when an Apgar index evaluation is conducted. The Apgar test provides a quick assessment of a newborn's overall health. It looks at five vital signs: the baby's color, pulse, reflexes, muscle tone, and breathing. Holly, a certified midwife, explains: "An Apgar test is done at one and five minutes [after birth]. I listen to the baby's heart and lungs with a stethoscope to make sure that the baby is breathing well, lungs are clear, and the heart rate is within a normal range."[20]

Based on the assessment, which is given twice and compared, the infant is given a score. A perfect score is ten. Newborns who score at least seven are considered healthy. The lower the score on the Apgar test, the more likely a problem exists.

Lung defects are usually detected during the Apgar evaluation, which can save a newborn's life. A lung defect can prevent a newborn from being able to breathe normally. When a lung defect is detected at birth, proper intervention is immediately administered. This keeps the baby from suffocating.

Depending where the baby is born, blood tests for other birth defects are also likely to be done. For example, every state in the United States requires that newborns are given a blood test that screens for phenylketonuria (PKU), a birth defect that hampers digestion. Colorado, Wisconsin, Wyoming, and Montana also administer a blood test on newborns that detects cystic fibrosis, and many states require newborns to be screened for sickle-cell anemia.

Other birth defects are often detected during a physical exam one to four days after a baby is born. The exam serves as a comprehensive evaluation of the infant. During the exam the infant's breathing and heart rate are monitored. The baby's muscles, head, neck, genitals, and anus are inspected for defects.

At this time premature infants are administered a head ultrasound. Since a premature infant's internal organs are often poorly developed, these babies are at a high risk of having undiscovered brain defects that a head ultrasound can detect. For instance, a problem like intraventricular hemorrhage (IVH), which is dangerous bleeding in the brain, can not only be detected by a head ultrasound, but the level of seriousness can also be determined or graded. This was how Jack's problem was detected. His mother explains: "Jack was less than forty-eight hours old when we were hit with a . . . bombshell—Jack had an intraventricular hemorrhage. The ultrasound showed grade 2. I went from feeling numb to worried and scared. What would this IVH mean to my child?"[21]

## Late Detection

Some birth defects like fragile X syndrome, muscular dystrophy, and cerebral palsy are not evident at birth, nor are they recognizable in infants. A child with cerebral palsy may never develop the ability to walk without assistance. However, since all infants are unable to walk, an infant with cerebral palsy appears to be normal. As the baby grows, a birth defect is suspected if he or she fails to acquire intellectual, motor, or speech skills on par with his or her peers. It is usually the parent who first notices a problem. Diane describes the delays her son exhibited: "When he started showing significant delays in normal developmental steps (rolled late, sat late, never crawled, wasn't potty trained, verbalized late, and walked late), I began questioning his pediatrician."[22]

When parents suspect a problem, a developmental evaluation is done. First the pediatrician compares the baby's progress to normal developmental milestones such as sitting by seven months and walking by fourteen months. Then, specialists evaluate the child. These specialists often include a neurologist who looks for nerve damage, an orthopedic specialist who examines the patient's bones and muscles, an audiologist who checks for hearing loss, and an ophthalmologist who looks for visual problems.

## A Wide Array of Treatments

No matter when a birth defect is detected, treatment usually begins once the problem is diagnosed. With five thousand different types of birth defects, treatments vary widely. Some treatments cannot be administered until an infant is strong enough to en-

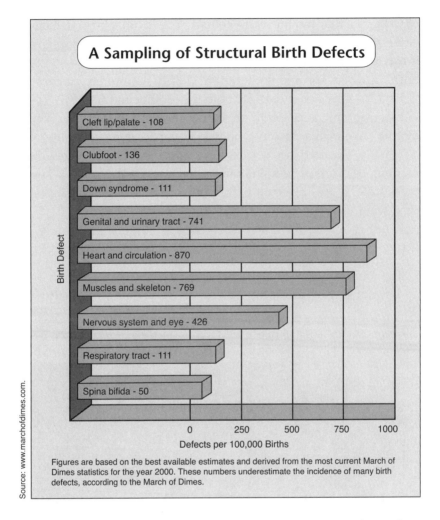

**A Sampling of Structural Birth Defects**

Cleft lip/palate - 108

Clubfoot - 136

Down syndrome - 111

Genital and urinary tract - 741

Heart and circulation - 870

Muscles and skeleton - 769

Nervous system and eye - 426

Respiratory tract - 111

Spina bifida - 50

Birth Defect

0    250    500    750    1000

Defects per 100,000 Births

Figures are based on the best available estimates and derived from the most current March of Dimes statistics for the year 2000. These numbers underestimate the incidence of many birth defects, according to the March of Dimes.

Source: www.marchofdimes.com.

dure them. Other treatments, like fetal surgery, are performed on unborn babies.

Fetal surgery involves treating a birth defect in a fetus. During fetal surgery an incision is made in the mother's abdomen. The fetus is carefully removed from the womb with the placenta still attached. This ensures that the fetus gets adequate oxygen and nutrition while out of the womb. Then, as in any type of surgery, the doctor repairs the problem. Among other procedures, this may involve sewing shut an opening on the fetus's back, in the case of spina bifida, or removing a life-threatening mass of cells called a cyst that can form on a fetus's lung in other birth defects. Afterward, the fetus is placed back in the womb to develop and grow, and the incision is sewn closed. The mother is kept in the hospital where she and the fetus are closely monitored.

Fetal surgery poses risks for both the mother and the fetus. Fetal surgery can cause death or premature birth of the fetus. The mother faces excess bleeding and infection. Therefore, fetal surgery is usually reserved for severe lung abnormalities, along with meningocele, a type of spina bifida that surgery can cure. When these defects are corrected before birth they are less damaging than when the defect is corrected after the baby is born.

A father, whose son Zane received fetal surgery for spina bifida, explains:

> The surgery was a relatively new surgery where the mother underwent surgery to expose the unborn baby; then a neurosur-

*Surgeons operate on the spine of a fetus with spina bifida. Although risky, fetal surgery is often less damaging than postnatal surgery.*

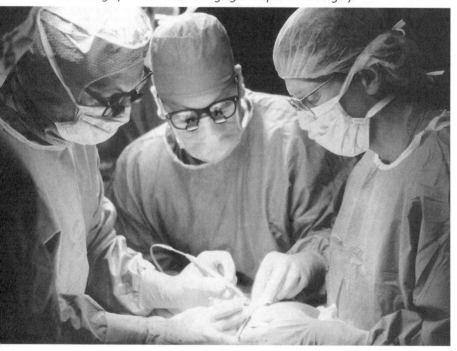

geon would carefully close the baby's back, just like what is normally done after a child with spina bifida is born. Then the fetus is then closed back inside the mother's womb, mother is sewn up, and the pregnancy continues. . . . By closing the defect early, and allowing the fetus to heal naturally in the uterus, neurological functions could be saved, hopefully allowing babies, which would normally not walk, urinate, and have malformed brains a chance at a more normal life. . . . Our baby underwent the fetal surgery. . . . Six and a half weeks later, Zane was born, kicking and screaming. . . . His lungs were terrific, and [he] was big for his early age. It appeared that both legs work perfectly and he is emptying his bladder on his own.[23]

## The Neonatal Intensive Care Unit

In most cases birth defects are not treated until after birth. When a newborn baby is diagnosed with a serious birth defect such as heart, kidney, or lung problems the infant is placed in the neonatal intensive care unit (NICU) of the hospital. Like the intensive care unit of a hospital, the NICU has a specially trained staff and special equipment designed to treat and monitor ill newborns.

Most babies in the NICU are kept in isolettes, small heated beds enclosed by clear plastic. Isolettes provide newborns with a warm quiet environment. Wires and tubes connect each baby to a variety of instruments that measure its heart rate, breathing, oxygen level, and blood pressure. For instance, wires attached to three electrodes placed on the baby's chest connect to a cardiorespiratory monitor, a machine that records the newborn's heart and breathing rates.

Babies that need help breathing may be attached to a ventilator. This machine pushes air in and out of the baby's lungs via a tube placed in the infant's windpipe and connected to the ventilator. Other tubes deliver medicine and food. Some newborns are administered medication intravenously. Among other things, such medication may be needed to help the baby's heart work, fight infection, or stimulate breathing. If the baby cannot take food normally, he or she is fed intravenously. A father recalls his daughter Rae's experience in NICU: "The array of monitors was astounding. At one time Rae had eleven things poking in her, on her, or out of her."[24]

While an infant is in the NICU, a nearby room is provided for its parents to sleep in. Babies stay in NICU until their lives are no longer at risk. This may be anywhere from a few days to several months.

## Surgical Intervention

Sometimes the only way to save an infant's life is with surgery to correct a birth defect. For example, infants born with hydrocephalus, a birth defect related to spina bifida, can die if the defect is not treated. When individuals have hydrocephalus, dangerous amounts of fluid gather in the blood vessels of the brain, causing the head to swell. But surgery, in which a tube called a shunt is placed in a blood vessel, moves the excess fluid out of the brain to the baby's abdomen. Here the fluid can drain without doing harm. Kim, Bailey's mother, remembers: "Bailey had to have a shunt at three weeks of age. . . . It was terrifying to watch such a fragile child head to the operating room. We were not sure if she would return. . . . [Today] watching Bailey laugh and play reminds me that she is a happy, healthy little girl."[25]

Heart, kidney, and digestive system problems are other birth defects commonly treated with surgery. Often surgery cures or diminishes the negative effects of the problem and the baby goes on to lead a happy life.

## Organ Transplants

Sometimes a baby is born with a heart, kidney, liver, or other organ that is so impaired that the only way to save the baby's life is through an organ transplant. At other times, damage from cystic fibrosis can cause a child's lungs to fail later in life, making an organ transplant necessary.

An organ transplant involves replacing a damaged organ with a healthy one taken from a recently deceased person. Organs must be matched to the recipient's body weight and blood type. Therefore, a baby with type B blood would need to receive an organ from another baby with type B blood because the immune system will reject a mismatched organ.

# A Record Surgery

Usually an organ transplant involves replacing one organ, but six-month-old Alessia di Matteo received eight organs in January 2004. Alessia was born with a birth defect that affects the way her stomach, pancreas, liver, small intestine, large intestine, kidneys, and spleen function. As a result of her problems, Alessia was very sick and spent most of her early life in the hospital. Doctors said that without organ transplants, she had no hope of survival, and they doubted whether Alessia could be kept alive long enough to go through eight different organ transplant surgeries. Her only hope was to have all eight organs transplanted at the same time. This had never been done before. But when doctors at Jackson Memorial Hospital in Miami, Florida, acquired all the organs Alessia needed from a seven-month-old donor, they decided to go ahead with the remarkable surgery.

According to an article by Coralie Carlson in the *Albuquerque Journal* recounting this remarkable surgery, "The 12-hour operation was performed in a space in the girl's abdomen about the size of three fists, and the organs transplanted weighed less than 11 ounces." Alessia came through the surgery well. As of March 20, 2004, "Alessia now weighs 13 pounds and is fed through a tube, but is out of the intensive care unit. . . . Doctors are monitoring her intestines, which are most likely to develop infections."

Both her doctors and her family are hopeful that she will not develop any infections or complications and that Alessia will be able to live a long, normal life.

Vital organs are taken from organ donors—people who had agreed that, upon their death, their organs were to be donated to others. Permission to take organs may also be granted by the families of the deceased. Unfortunately, there are many more people in need of donated organs than there are organs available. So, sick children are put on a waiting list until a suitable organ is found. Yvette, whose daughter Bianka had a heart transplant, recalls: "The doctors told me it could take a week or months for a match to come in. They also told me she could die waiting."[26]

When a match is found, the organ is removed from the donor's body and put in cold storage where it can survive for about four hours. While the donated organ is in transport, the transplant team gets ready. This group includes a pediatric transplant surgeon, a respiratory therapist, an anesthesiologist, and nurses specially trained in transplant surgery.

Once the team is ready, the patient is prepared for surgery. Anesthesia is administered. As soon as the patient is asleep a breathing tube is inserted into his or her windpipe. Another tube is inserted into a vein in the patient's neck. This tube monitors oxygen levels in the patient's blood. Then the surgeon makes an incision, which allows access to the organ. For example, in heart transplant surgery an incision is made in the patient's chest from the neck to above the abdomen. Blood supply to the organ is shut off so the surgeon can work. Usually this involves putting clamps on the blood vessels that bring blood to the organ. In the case of heart transplants, the blood vessels are connected to a heart-lung machine that takes over the heart's pumping action. Once this is done the old organ is removed and the new organ is put carefully in its place. The organ is then connected to the blood vessels, and the clamps or heart-lung machine are removed. If all goes well, the new organ starts working immediately and the incision is sewn closed.

Transplant surgery often saves young patients' lives. The mother of Dan, a child with cystic fibrosis who needed a lung transplant to survive, explains:

> He struggled for each breath he took. He couldn't eat because he was so weak and coughing made him vomit. He couldn't walk

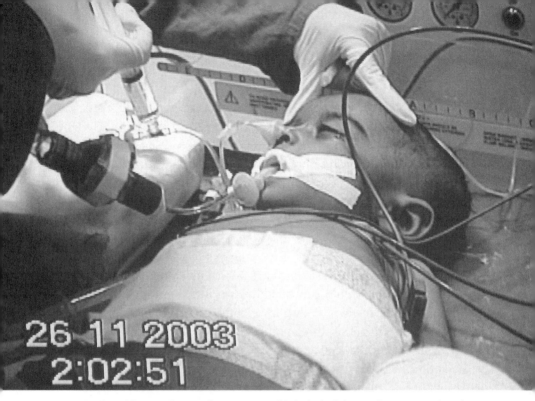

26 11 2003
2:02:51

*During videotaped transplant surgery, this baby's defective liver was replaced with part of his uncle's liver, saving the child's life.*

and he slept a great deal of the time. . . . When he was admitted [to the hospital] . . . his doctor told us things were very serious. . . . His only hope was a transplant. I prayed for a miracle and within days, healthy lungs became available for transplant. . . .

Thankfully, the surgery was a great success. . . . I still find it hard to believe the transformation that has occurred with Dan. He is doing extremely well. He doesn't cough anymore. He is growing stronger everyday. He can actually walk to the mailbox and ride his bike. He has been fishing with his brother and will be returning to school.[27]

## Ongoing Treatments

Currently, some birth defects cannot be repaired. Incurable birth defects include muscular dystrophy, cystic fibrosis, cerebral palsy, Down syndrome, fetal alcohol syndrome, some forms of spina bifida, and sickle-cell anemia. For individuals with these birth defects, ongoing treatments help control the effects of the disorder. For example, with every meal, individuals with cystic fibrosis must take a pill that allows them to digest food. This medicine replaces natural digestive enzymes. Without this medicine people with cystic fibrosis can become malnourished and die. Therefore, this enzyme must be taken throughout these individuals' lives.

Individuals with sickle-cell anemia also take long-term medication. This disease weakens the body, making it especially vulnerable to infection. This is particularly a problem for young children whose immune systems are not as developed as those of adults. A common cold can quickly turn into a life-threatening case of pneumonia in a young sickle-cell patient. To help prevent what can become a life-threatening infection, children under the age of six with sickle-cell anemia are administered a daily dose of an antibiotic. Many people with the disease also take frequent doses of pain medication. These include over-the-counter medications such as aspirin, or stronger prescription medications such as codeine and morphine.

Unfortunately, all medications can cause side effects and health risks. Taking medication on a long-term basis can increase negative effects. Long-term use of antibiotics, for example, can cause damage to helpful bacteria that live in the body and are needed for digestion. Pain medications can cause stomach ulcers and damage the liver and kidneys. Prescription pain medicine can be addictive. However, since ongoing treatments with these and other medications can save life as well as improve its quality, many people with birth defects feel the benefits of these medications outweigh the risks.

It is clear that there are many ways to diagnose and treat birth defects. While some birth defects can be diagnosed and treated before a baby is born, some children with birth defects must wait months or even years before their problem is identified. However, with proper treatment, many of these conditions are curable. Even when a cure is impossible, ongoing treatments can make life better for people with birth defects.

# Chapter 3

# Living with Birth Defects

L IVING WITH A birth defect can be challenging. Among the challenges individuals cope with are motor and communication skills; limited mobility; strength; learning disabilities; and persistent fatigue. There are a variety of ways people meet these challenges. In so doing they improve the quality of their lives.

## The Challenge of Limited Mobility

Birth defects such as cerebral palsy, spina bifida, muscular dystrophy, or missing limbs can affect an individual's ability to walk. This means that affected individuals may have to depend on others to help them get around, limiting their freedom and independence. In fact, without the assistance of others these individuals may be confined to their beds. Using special equipment such as braces, crutches, and wheelchairs helps these people to overcome their impairment and be more independent.

Braces are made of lightweight plastic that are attached to Velcro strips which wrap securely around a person's limbs. They are worn over an individual's foot, ankle, leg, or hip, and are custom made to fit each individual perfectly. As an individual's limbs grow and change, braces are replaced.

Because they fit securely, braces support, stabilize, and stretch weak muscles, allowing people with limited mobility to use their feet, ankles, and legs more easily. The mother of Jimmy, an eighteen-month-old child with cerebral palsy, recalls:

> He began wearing the braces on February 12, 1996 and started standing for a few seconds at a time by February 17, 1996. . . .

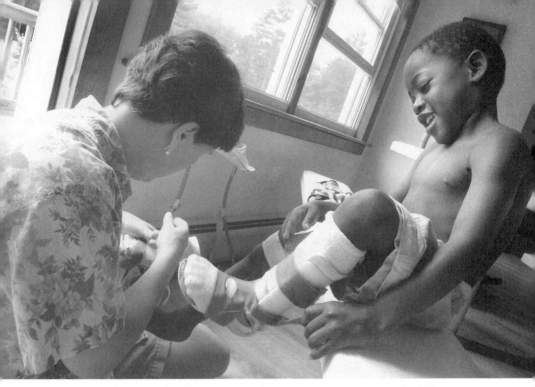

*This boy, born with cerebral palsy, can walk only with the help of braces. Braces, crutches, and wheelchairs help children with certain defects to get around.*

On February 19, 1996, Jimmy took his first steps! . . . He was standing and holding onto a little wooden table and moved his feet, just like anybody else, and took steps . . . I am calling them steps, but it was more like what an eight-month-old would do along a table or couch. However, it was a whole lot more than Jimmy had done before.[28]

## Crutches

Crutches are another tool that helps people meet the challenge of limited mobility. Often they are used in combination with braces. People with cerebral palsy, spina bifida, and muscular dystrophy use crutches that have metal rings similar to bracelets that fit securely around the wearer's arms to provide stability. The metal rings are padded on the inside to make them comfortable. Because crutches provide people with support and balance, many mobility-challenged individuals are able to walk with their assistance. Jimmy's mother remembers: "Two days after we brought the crutches home, Jimmy walked. . . . This was the first time that his balance was good enough. He saw himself in a mirror, smiled big, and said, 'Hello Jimmy.' We all clapped and cried."[29]

## Wheelchairs

Some individuals' mobility is so limited that they cannot walk even with the help of braces or crutches. Other individuals turn to a wheelchair so their hands are free to do things like housework, shopping, or cooking. Still others use a wheelchair in public places such as college campuses, museums, airports, sports arenas, and shopping malls. Because of their size, these places can be difficult for people with limited mobility to get around in without the help of a wheelchair.

Wheelchairs vary in size and design and can be manual or motorized. Individuals roll the wheels of manual wheelchairs with their arms. Motorized wheelchairs are useful for people with

*Electric wheelchairs allow even severely disabled people like this woman to participate in normal activities, such as attending a baseball game.*

# Assistance Dogs

Assistance dogs are specially trained dogs that help people with a variety of birth defects face the challenges of daily living. An article on the Special Child Web site explains what these dogs do: "An 'assistance dog' is any dog who helps a person with a physical, cognitive, or seizure related disability or illness, including, but not limited to blindness, deafness, cerebral palsy, or epilepsy."

Assistance dogs act as helpers and companions. The dogs and the individuals they assist are considered part-

*A specially trained service dog licks the face of his companion, a young boy with cerebral palsy.*

cerebral palsy or muscular dystrophy who may have limited use of their hands and arms, as well as for people who need to traverse large distances each day. These wheelchairs have a small electric motor, which is controlled with a handle or joystick. Both manual and motorized wheelchairs allow people with disabling birth defects to do what nondisabled people can do. Jesse Paul, a young man with cerebral palsy, explains:

ners since they work together as a team. There are a number of different types of assistance dogs. Dogs of each type are trained for different jobs. Guide dogs are probably the most widely known type of assistance dog. Guide dogs help visually impaired people by acting as their partners' eyes. They are responsible for their partners' safety. They guide their partners through traffic, crowded streets; and around the house. They are taught to cross streets, stop at stairs, traffic lights, and curbs; and lead their owners around obstacles in their path. Labrador retrievers, golden retrievers, and German shepherds all make good guide dogs.

Hearing dogs help hearing-impaired people. They act like their partners' ears. These dogs nudge or prod their partners to alert them to important sounds. Then they lead their partners to the sound. Sounds from a telephone, doorbell, or a smoke alarm are a few of these sounds.

Service dogs are trained to help people with physical disabilities. These dogs pull wheelchairs, help people up when they have fallen, carry items in their mouths, retrieve items, press elevator buttons, open and close doors, turn light switches on and off, help people get dressed, and bark for help when it is needed. Some service dogs also are trained to alert a partner who is about to have a seizure. According to the Special Child Web site, "These dogs can actually predict when the person is going to have a seizure by smelling changes in the body chemistry."

I still use crutches, but I have a wheelchair to go places that would normally be too much distance, and to help me do things around the house. I tried to do some things without the wheelchair when I left home to go to college and got my apartment, but after walking around campus and finding you have to have both hands to do things (especially in the kitchen when you're cooking), it makes it much easier and faster.[30]

## The Role of Physical Therapy

Participating in a physical therapy program is another way individuals improve their mobility and reach the maximum level of their physical potential. Depending on the person and his or her disability, this may range from gaining the skills to get in and out of a wheelchair to developing the ability to walk, climb stairs, or even run without special equipment.

Specially trained health care professionals, known as physical therapists, help disabled individuals achieve their goals. They do this through the use of individually customized exercises that

*Physical therapy helps many people with birth defects. Here, a therapist beats on the chest of a child with cystic fibrosis to loosen mucus and help her to breathe more easily.*

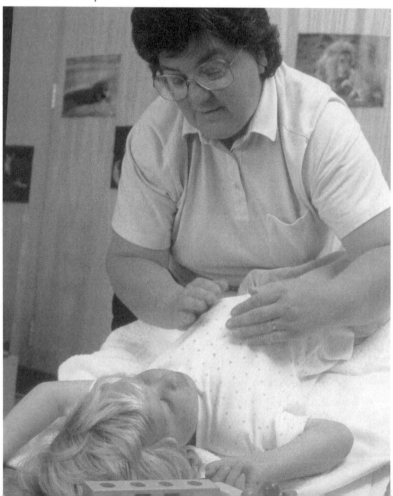

concentrate on stretching and strengthening leg muscles. As a result, the person's balance, flexibility, muscle control, and endurance all improve.

Physical therapy sessions are usually held at least twice a week for thirty minutes per session. They take place in physical therapy centers that resemble a gym with weight-training machines, pulleys, exercise bicycles, and massage tables. There individuals go through their personal exercises under the supervision of physical therapists. When clients cannot move their muscles on their own, the physical therapists move and manipulate the muscles for them.

Physical therapists also provide their clients with exercise routines to do at home. The combination of physical therapy sessions and home exercises can take up a large part of a person's life. Christopher, an eleven-year-old with muscular dystrophy, follows this schedule: "From 7:30 to 8 in the morning, he does leg exercises and manual stretches at home; then at a quarter to 9 he gets more stretches at school, at 12:30 more stretches, more when he gets off the bus and then again before bed. On the days when he has PT [physical therapy] after school, he goes from school to therapy."[31]

## Physical Therapy to Improve Breathing

In addition to improving mobility, physical therapy helps individuals with cystic fibrosis and other lung impairments improve their ability to breathe. This makes it easier for them to perform daily activities and be active.

In a process known as chest physical therapy or chest percussion, an individual lies in various positions on his or her back and chest. The physical therapist gently thumps the person's back or chest with cupped hands. This loosens and dislodges mucus in the airways, which is coughed up, allowing the individual to breathe more easily.

Chest physical therapy is done anywhere from one to four times a day depending on the patient's needs. Because of its frequency, physical therapists often visit clients at home at a convenient time that does not disrupt their patients' school or work schedule. Sometimes a family member is trained to perform the procedure.

## The Challenge of Poor Motor Skills

People with cerebral palsy, muscular dystrophy, or Down syndrome can have difficulty using their hands and fingers. Among other things, dressing, grooming, eating, writing, turning the pages of a book, and cooking can present challenges for these individuals and for people with missing limbs. Participating in occupational therapy helps them meet these challenges.

Occupational therapy is similar to physical therapy, but it concentrates on developing small muscles in the hands, as well as improving eye-hand coordination. Through a variety of activities that simulate real-life tasks, an occupational therapist helps people to develop and control weak muscles and to use strong muscles in place of or to assist weaker ones. This may be through guided and repeated practice in an activity such as opening and closing a zipper, or through play therapy in which fun activities help develop impaired body parts. For example, the therapist may spray shaving cream on a mirror and ask the client to make a snowman. This develops eye-hand coordination and stretches muscles in the hands and fingers. The end result is that individuals with impaired motor skills are better able to participate as fully as possible in their home, school, and work lives.

## Coping with Communication Challenges

Some birth defects affect the ability to communicate. Individuals with hearing loss face challenges in learning language and communicating with others. Because it is difficult for them to express their wants and needs and to interact with others, they often become isolated. Learning is also hard for these individuals. For example, hearing children learn how to speak by listening to others. But with deaf children this is not possible. One way some people with hearing loss cope is by using a hearing aid, which can help some, but not all, deaf people.

Babies as young as two months can be fitted with a hearing aid. A hearing aid is usually worn in the ear, or behind the ear, attached to a plastic earmold inside the ear. A hearing aid does not restore a person's hearing. Instead, it amplifies sound. This is done when a tiny microphone inside the hearing aid changes sound into electrical energy. The electrical signal is then sent to a receiver that converts the electrical signal to amplified sound. This helps connect a hearing-impaired person with the world around him or her. It also makes it possible for a young child to hear spoken language and thus develop language skills. The mother of Jill, a two-year-old born with hearing loss, states: "Jill got her first set of hearing aids when she was six months old. . . . She began by wearing them five minutes every hour, and we very slowly increased her time . . . until she was wearing them all the time. . . . She is happy, healthy, and communicating with me now."[32]

## Speech Therapy

Whereas hearing aids help individuals to hear better, speech therapy helps people to communicate more effectively. Hearing loss, cerebral palsy, fragile X syndrome, and Down syndrome often cause speech impairments. Because of speech impairments,

*Hearing aids help this boy compensate for a congenital hearing impairment. Also, speech therapy helps him to communicate intelligibly with others.*

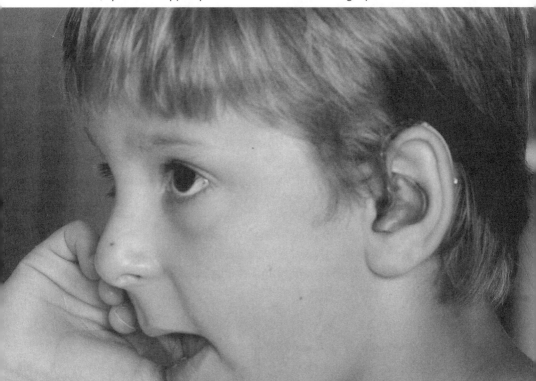

many people with these birth defects have trouble being understood. This can be quite frustrating.

Lisa, an educator who works with children with speech impairments, explains: "Everyone should have the opportunity to express themselves and make choices for themselves in this life. How would you feel if you couldn't tell someone something as simple as what you would like to wear today or whether or not you want breakfast, not to mention to not be able to tell someone if you are sick, hurt or afraid?"[33]

Speech therapy helps people deal with this challenge. During speech therapy sessions, a speech therapist instructs individuals on how to position the tongue and mouth so that the basic sounds that form words can be produced more clearly. The speech therapist can also help clients to improve the rhythm and tone of their speech, expand their vocabularies, and put words together in the proper sequence.

## Sign Language

Sign language gives people who have difficulty speaking another way to communicate. Commonly used by the deaf, it is also an important tool for people with cerebral palsy and Down syndrome who may not be able to speak well. Sign language is a visible language in which speakers make specific signs with their fingers and hands to communicate words and sentences. Deaf children whose parents are also deaf learn sign language in the same way hearing children learn oral language—by imitating their parents. Other children are often taught sign language by a speech therapist.

Sign language allows individuals who cannot express themselves clearly to be understood and provides a means for hearing people to communicate with nonhearing individuals. This reduces feelings of isolation and frustration caused by the inability to communicate with others. According to members of DEAF.com, a group that represents deaf people, "Deaf people in the United States and Canada have found that ASL [American Sign Language] affords them an immediate means of communication and a source of enrichment and freedom. A means of liberation, if you will."[34]

*These hearing-impaired children are learning sign language with the help of their teacher and a computer program.*

## Assistive Communication Equipment

New technology also helps people communicate without speaking. Computers with special software can change typed words to spoken words with the use of a synthesizer. Some have a head pointer that lets people with severe motor impairments type on the computer keyboard without the using their hands. Most head pointers look like helmets with a long pointer attached. Individuals type by moving the pointer along the keyboard with their heads.

Most communication equipment is small enough to be held in a person's lap or mounted on a wheelchair. This gives users the means to communicate wherever they go. Therefore, they can be involved in activities that they might otherwise be excluded from. Pati, a woman with muscular dystrophy who uses this type of device, says that because of it: "I will always be able to express what I am thinking. I will always have a way to say no or yes. I will always have a way to say I require assistance. . . . [I] remain in control of my life."[35]

# Swimming as Therapy and Sport

For many people with birth defects, exercising in water is an important part of their lives. Exercising in water is therapeutic. It improves an individual's breathing, circulation, balance, muscle strength, and flexibility. And since the buoyancy of water supports a person and minimizes the effects of gravity, it provides people who ordinarily cannot move easily on land with a sense of freedom. As a result, many people with muscular dystrophy, cerebral palsy, and spina bifida frequently attend special swimming and water exercise classes for people with disabilities.

Some, like Kara Sheridan, participate in swim meets competing against other disabled individuals. Kara is a twenty-four-year-old woman with brittle bone disorder, a birth defect that causes her bones to break easily and confines her to a wheelchair. Although she has had more than

## Facing the Challenge of Limited Strength and Fatigue

Individuals with cystic fibrosis, sickle-cell anemia, muscular dystrophy, and heart defects often are not as strong as other people and tire easily. Lack of stamina makes performing even small tasks difficult. Going to school or work, doing chores, and visiting with friends all can seem overwhelming. Getting adequate rest and eating a healthy balanced diet are two ways people cope with this challenge. While important for everyone, it is especially important that individuals with fatiguing birth defects get enough sleep and proper nutrition; otherwise, they may not have enough stamina to function adequately.

Sleep helps renew and strengthen the body. People facing persistent fatigue find that taking short naps during the day and get-one hundred broken bones in her life and weighs only eighty-two pounds, Kara set the disabled world record in the two-hundred-meter breaststroke in 2004 and qualified to be a member of the 2004 U.S. Paraolympic team.

Kara trains twice a day, seven days a week, swimming about three miles each day. In order to strengthen her bones, Kara started therapeutic swimming as an infant. An article by Michelle Kaufman in the *Albuquerque Journal* explains:

> She started as an infant, at the advice of doctors. In a few years, she was doing backflips underwater, pretending to be a gymnast. . . .
>
> Sheridan says swimming is liberating.
>
> "I spent most of my life maintaining and fixing my body, and I never imagined my body could go faster than another person at anything," she said. "It makes me feel so good, gives me so much confidence."

ting eight hours of sleep each night help them to cope. So too does accepting their limitations and taking rest periods and breaks whenever necessary. A young man with muscular dystrophy explains: "I pace myself. I don't try to overdo it."[36]

Eating a healthy diet also helps combat fatigue and increase strength. Foods such as meat, chicken, and fish, rich in protein, and dairy products, high in calcium, build and strengthen muscles and bones. Complex carbohydrates in cereals, rice, pasta, and breads provide the body with energy. Vitamins and minerals in fruits and vegetables fight infection. Therefore, eating a diet rich in these foods gives people more strength and energy.

## Exercise for Strength and Energy

Participating in mild exercise also strengthens the body and fights fatigue. When people exercise, their bodies release endorphins, natural chemicals that give exercisers a sense of relaxation and wellness. Such feelings help combat fatigue.

Exercise also strengthens muscles and joints, which makes tackling any activity easier. In addition, exercise helps individuals with fetal alcohol syndrome, who are often hyperactive, release nervous energy and gain control over their behavior.

Swimming, yoga, and horseback riding are some of the most popular forms of exercise that people with disabilities participate in. Chad, a twenty-six-year-old with muscular dystrophy and an avid swimmer, attributes his strength and energy to swimming. He says: "I'm probably one of the strongest people with MD [muscular dystrophy] that I know. I'm stronger than people that are 18 years old. . . . [I] think swimming is the best."[37]

## Coping with Educational Challenges

Individuals with learning, mobility, and motor impairments all face challenges in school. Those with learning disabilities do not learn in the same way nondisabled people do. The normal classroom may be too fast paced to meet their needs. Mobility problems make it hard to navigate crowded school hallways, climb stairs, and get in and out of school chairs. Taking notes, completing assignments and exams on time, raising hands, and carrying heavy books all present challenges to people with motor impairments. Allyson's mother explains how weak hand muscles caused by muscular dystrophy challenge her daughter in school: "With Allyson her pencil [feels like it] weighs about ten pounds after she uses it a while."[38]

A number of laws require schools to make modifications to enable students with disabilities to meet these challenges. Such modifications include access to elevators and ramps, more accommodating chairs, reduced assignments, extended deadlines, and access to equipment that makes learning easier. For instance, Allyson uses a computer with a touch pad to help her to write. Touch pads allow users who do not have enough strength in their hands to manipulate the computer mouse to simply drag a fingertip across an electronic pad. Allyson explains: "I use my computer every time I have a story to write or an essay, any kind of work in the book that you have to copy, anything that you have to write out the answers for."[39]

In addition, many disabled students are assigned a one-on-one educational aide to whom they can dictate their work. The aide also helps the students move from class to class and take notes, among other things. Ian, a young man with motor impairments, says: "I had the same assistant all through high school. She took notes, transcribed whatever I would dictate to her, organized my books. . . . All in all, it's way better than if I tried to do it on my own. We were like a well oiled machine."[40]

Some students attend special education classes. Here, specially trained teachers work with students in a slower-paced environment, providing them with instruction designed to meet their individual needs and abilities. This includes instruction in academic subjects as well as motor and communication skills. An early childhood special education teacher explains:

> My day is set up much like any other classroom you might see in which children are learning elementary, basic skills. The big difference is that we have to also work on daily living skills

*Many disabled students learn with the help of specially designed equipment, such as this computer mouse and keyboard.*

such as eating, walking, playing, and using the ever popular bathroom. We also work on academics such as colors, numbers, and name identification. . . . Independence is the battle cry around here. Anything a child can do by themselves, they are encouraged to do.[41]

## Getting Support from People with Similar Problems

Sometimes people with birth defects feel isolated and different from nondisabled people who do not fully understand the challenges they face. Becoming acquainted with people who face similar challenges allows individuals with birth defects to share their feelings, experiences, and problems. Joining a support group is one way to do this.

There are support groups for every kind of birth defect. In these groups members share information and encouragement with each other. In so doing they feel less isolated and are able to work toward solutions to problems that people without their particular birth defect do not face.

To name just a few, health organizations like the Cystic Fibrosis Foundation, the Muscular Dystrophy Association, and the American Heart Association sponsor local support groups. These groups can be found throughout the United States and welcome people of all ages. There are even electronic support groups that share information via the Internet.

## Summer Camps

Special summer camps allow children and teens with birth defects to gather with other young people who share their disability. These summer camps give young people with a specific disorder the opportunity to have fun and interact with others like themselves in a safe environment. Supervised by specially trained counselors and health care professionals, campers participate in physical activities, share experiences, and attend educational sessions in which they learn more about their disorder. The experiences campers have help them to feel more independent and self-confident. This helps them to better cope with the challenges they face in their daily lives.

*A disabled youngster smiles as she competes in a swimming event in the 2003 Special Olympics Games in Vermont.*

In an article about Camp del Corazon, a summer camp for children with heart defects, camp chief executive Glen Knight states: "Just a simple activity such as swimming or hiking that we take for granted is an unbelievable experience for these children." The article goes on to explain: "Many children did not know, until they came to Camp del Corazon, what it feels like to do these activities. And this participation has helped them to overcome some of the self consciousness . . . they often carry around with them."[42]

It is clear that people with birth defects face many challenges. By taking steps to meet these challenges, individuals with birth defects are able to reach their goals and lead happy, productive lives. That is exactly what Jimmy, a fifteen-year-old honor student with spina bifida, is doing. His mother says: "He touches the lives of almost everyone he knows because of his brave determination to meet the challenges of everyday life. . . . He realized early in life that things may be difficult, but that life is good and worth the fight, that he controls his quality of life. He has set many goals for himself, many of which he has already achieved. I know he will reach them all!"[43]

# Chapter 4

# Preventing Birth Defects

NOT ALL BIRTH defects are preventable, but many are. By taking a number of steps, prospective parents can defend their offspring against preventable birth defects. Among these steps are getting genetic counseling, receiving proper prenatal care, eating right, taking adequate folic acid, and making healthy lifestyle choices.

## Genetic Counseling

Undergoing genetic counseling is one step that helps prevent birth defects. Genetic counseling allows a couple to learn whether one or both of them carry the gene for a particular birth defect and, therefore, whether their child will carry the gene or actually have the defect. Genetic counseling is especially important for people at high risk of having a child with a birth defect. This group includes individuals with a family history of an inherited disorder, those from certain ethnic groups, parents with a birth defect, as well as those who already have a child with a birth defect.

During genetic counseling prospective parents meet with a specially trained health care professional known as a genetic counselor. The genetic counselor gathers information that helps determine how the couple's health may affect their baby. This information includes the mother's age; the state of each partner's health; their ethnicity; what, if any, medications or drugs the mother uses; and whether either partner has a family history of inherited diseases or birth defects. Then the counselor evaluates the information and discusses it with the pair. A father whose oldest daughter was born without fingers on her left hand recalls:

> Before we had our younger daughter, we went to a genetic counselor to find out what the chances were that she would be born with the same problem as her sister. We didn't know what caused it, and we kept blaming ourselves. The genetic counselor explained that being born without fingers wasn't genetic. She told us that it randomly happens to 1 in 4000 infants, and that our second daughter was as likely or unlikely to be born that way as any baby anywhere. That was a relief.[44]

*A couple hoping to have a child speaks with a genetic counselor. Such counseling can prevent defects by alerting parents to genetic health issues.*

Next, in order to find out if either parent carries a faulty gene for sickle-cell anemia, cystic fibrosis, thalassemia, or Tay-Sachs disease, blood tests are administered. Using these results and the data collected through the medical history, the counselor establishes the chances that the baby will have a birth defect. Bonnie recalls:

*A couple likely to have a child with a birth defect should learn all they can about the defect before planning a pregnancy.*

The counselor talked to us and took our medical history. I told the counselor that I was born with six fingers and toes on each of my hands and feet. The counselor explained that I carry the gene for extra fingers and toes, but my husband does not. So, there was a 50 percent chance our baby would be born with extra fingers or toes too. Then she told us our baby was at risk for Tay-Sachs disease. She sent us for blood work to find out if we had the gene; neither of us had it.[45]

## Looking at Alternatives

If the test results indicate that a couple is likely to have a child with a birth defect, the genetic counselor provides the couple with information about the birth defect. This includes what the baby's chances of survival are; what medical problems a child with the defect faces; what the child's future is likely to hold; and what physical, mental, and social challenges the child may face. Parents can prepare for having a child with a birth defect by learning as much as they can about the disorder before the child is born. This includes contacting health and social organizations that might help them, as well as talking to parents whose children face the same challenge. If the couple feels that they do not want to bring a child with a birth defect into the world, the genetic counselor helps them to explore other options.

If the female is already pregnant, one option is an abortion, which terminates the pregnancy. "I just don't think it's right to bring another child into the world with a chronic disease if you can help it," Shaniqua explains. She and her partner Keeshawn found out in genetic counseling that they are sickle-cell anemia carriers.

Keeshawn continues: "Yeah, that's my feeling too. Shaniqua and I have decided that when she gets pregnant, we'll have prenatal testing. If the fetus tests positive for sickle cell disease, she'll have an abortion. It's not fair to bring a child into the world who's going to suffer so much, and who might have a shorter life after all that suffering."[46]

An abortion is a personal and emotional decision. It is also controversial. Many people object to abortion on ethical and religious grounds, and there are those who say that children with birth defects can live fulfilling lives. Other people feel that abortion is the most humane choice.

## Additional Choices

One option for parents who have not yet conceived is adoption. Adoption allows high-risk couples to parent a healthy child. Shaniqua says: "If we decide that we can't have at biological child, there are so many kids in the world who need a loving home. We can adopt one."[47]

If prospective parents prefer to have a biological child, in vitro fertilization is another choice. In vitro fertilization involves medical professionals removing eggs from the female and sperm from the male. The eggs are fertilized with the sperm in a laboratory and placed in a test tube. When a fertilized egg starts dividing, cells from the egg are removed and analyzed for genetic disorders. If the fertilized egg is free of faulty genes, it is implanted in the woman's womb where it develops normally.

## Ensuring a Healthy Pregnancy

In addition to genetic counseling, there are other steps individuals can take to protect their baby. One is planning the pregnancy rather than allowing it to occur unexpectedly.

When a pregnancy is planned, the mother can take action even before she becomes pregnant to ensure that her baby is safeguarded from preventable birth defects. For instance, getting a thorough checkup before pregnancy is a good way to evaluate the woman's overall health and determine whether her body is ready to sustain a healthy pregnancy. During the checkup all vaccinations are brought up to date. This protects the baby from the *Rubella* and chicken pox viruses since, if the mother gets these diseases during pregnancy, they can cause defects in the fetus. At the same time, the woman is screened and treated for sexually transmitted diseases. This protects the fetus against the damaging effects of these illnesses. A new mother recalls her experience:

> When my husband and I decided to try to become pregnant . . . I wanted to take every step to ensure that our child-to-be was given every advantage in this harsh world, and I wanted to know what

*Discussing the harmful effects of certain medications with their physician can help pregnant women minimize the risk of birth defects.*

we could do in the pre-conception days to give him that boost. . . . I scheduled an appointment with my doctor, telling her we were going to start trying to conceive and asking her for tests and preparation-advice. . . . I had blood drawn to make sure that I was immunized against Rubella. . . . A week-or-so later all of the test results were in, and I was "cleared for pregnancy."[48]

Planning a pregnancy also gives a woman time to clear the harmful effects of medications, illegal drugs, dangerous chemicals, and alcohol from her body before she becomes pregnant. It provides an overweight woman a chance to lose weight before her unhealthy weight can cause problems for the fetus. It also allows a woman who normally does not eat well to get into the habit of eating a healthy diet. Indeed, planning and getting ready for pregnancy is so important that the Texas Medical Association urges women, "Take some important steps to prepare yourself for pregnancy. Taking care of your body before, as well as during, pregnancy provides the best prevention of future health problems in your baby."[49]

## Getting Prenatal Care

Once a woman is pregnant, getting adequate prenatal care is another way to prevent many birth defects. A pregnant woman needs to see a health care professional once a month for the first eight weeks of pregnancy, and once every two or three weeks thereafter. These visits allow the doctor to monitor the health of

# Exercise and Rest

Pregnant women are encouraged to exercise during pregnancy. Moderate exercise like yoga, walking, biking, and swimming helps strengthen a woman's body, which is good for the fetus. However, some forms of exercise can be risky. Weight lifting, for example, can harm the fetus. So too can lifting heavy objects around the house. This is because heavy lifting puts pressure on the uterus where the fetus is housed. Extra pressure on the uterus can make it contract and lead to premature labor and birth.

In fact, any physical activity, if it is overdone, can stress the mother and fetus. That is why it is important that pregnant women get adequate rest. Sleep is the body's way to reenergize and strengthen itself. When a woman is pregnant her body works extra hard to care for the baby developing inside her. This causes pregnant women to fatigue easily. Getting adequate rest helps expectant mothers to fight fatigue and maintain their strength, energy, and health. Stronger, healthier mothers are better equipped to provide the fetus with an optimal environment in which to develop. Indeed, rest appears to increase blood flow to the fetus, providing the developing infant with maximum levels of oxygen and nutrition.

*Mothers-to-be need adequate rest as well as regular, moderate exercise to maintain their own health and that of their baby.*

the mother and the fetus. Problems in the pregnancy that can cause birth defects are likely to be discovered during these visits. In some cases the problems can be treated and cured before the baby is born.

During these visits the expectant mother is educated about what warning signs to look for indicating something is wrong. These include vaginal bleeding, abdominal pain, blurred vision, dizziness, fainting, and swollen hands and face. The mother is told to seek immediate medical care if these symptoms appear. This may help prevent a birth defect and save the baby's life. For example, vaginal bleeding frequently precedes premature labor, which can be prevented with bed rest and medication if treatment begins soon enough. Maternal fainting can be caused by circulatory problems. If such problems are not treated, the fetus may not get adequate blood and oxygen, a problem that can lead to fetal death or birth defects like cerebral palsy. Blurred vision and dizziness are signs of anemia; this means that the mother's blood lacks iron. The body uses iron to manufacture red blood cells that carry food and oxygen to every cell in the mother's and the fetus's body. Lack of iron leads to abnormal fetal brain development. With proper prenatal care, the mother can be given an iron supplement that prevents this problem.

The mother is also given tips on how to best handle the discomforts of pregnancy, as well as what lifestyle changes she should make in order to safeguard her health and the health of the fetus. Indeed, according to Planned Parenthood, adequate prenatal care can help reduce the risk of premature and low-birthweight births, and the complications they cause, by 300 percent.

## Preventing Birth Defects with Good Nutrition

Even if a pregnancy is unplanned, an expectant mother can still take action that limits her baby's chances of developing a preventable birth defect. Among the most important actions is ensuring that the fetus gets proper nutrition by eating a healthy, well-balanced diet, as well as avoiding certain foods that can harm the fetus. Among these foods are shark, swordfish, mackerel, albacore tuna, and tilefish. These fish often live in polluted waters where they absorb methylmercury and other toxins through their skin. Over time, the toxins build up in the fatty tissue of the fish. When a pregnant woman eats these fish, the fetus is exposed to the toxins.

According to a 2000 report by the National Academy of Sciences, such exposure causes approximately sixty thousand neurological birth defects each year. Therefore, in 2004 the U.S. Food and Drug Administration and the Environmental Protection Agency recommended that women who might become pregnant and women who are pregnant not eat shark, swordfish, mackerel, or tilefish, and eat no more than six ounces of albacore tuna a week.

## Avoiding Other Dangerous Foods

Similarly, pregnant women should avoid foods that frequently harbor food-poisoning pathogens. The Food and Drug Administration warns pregnant women to avoid hot dogs and lunch meat, soft cheeses, meat spreads, unpasteurized milk, raw or undercooked meat, and raw sprouts, all of which can shelter germs that are linked to life-threatening birth defects.

Liver too is avoided. Liver contains high quantities of vitamin A. While vitamin A is needed for normal fetal growth, fetal exposure to more than ten thousand international units (IU) of the vitamin each day has been linked to babies being born with heart defects, cleft lips and palates, and hydrocephalus. A three-ounce serving of beef liver contains thirty thousand IU of vitamin A. Although it has not been proven that eating liver causes birth defects, there is a strong possibility that if a pregnant woman eats liver regularly she is putting her baby at risk. Therefore, in order

*Pregnant women should avoid foods such as these lunch meats, which are known to harbor pathogens linked to birth defects.*

to prevent the possibility of birth defects developing, many pregnant women avoid consuming liver.

## Harmful Beverages

In a like manner, many pregnant women are cautious about what they drink. In order to avoid fetal alcohol syndrome, they avoid all alcoholic drinks. They also avoid excess caffeine. Having more than two cups of a caffeinated beverage each day has been linked to premature and low-weight births.

Herbal teas can also be risky. Many herbs have medicinal properties. In fact, some herbs can be as potent as drugs. Scientists do not yet know what effect exposure to different herbs has on a developing fetus. In order to guard the fetus from any damage that some herbs may do, many women avoid herbal teas and nonvitamin supplements during pregnancy. Dietician and author Bridget Swinney warns: "We just don't know enough about the effect of herbs during pregnancy, so it makes sense to play it safe and stick with decaf black tea or flavored tea."[50]

## Folic Acid

In order for the fetus to develop normally, it is important that an expectant mother get adequate vitamin B9, or folic acid. It is one of the most vital nutrients for preventing neural tube defects. Indeed, studies have shown that 50 to 70 percent of all neural tube defects can be prevented if women consume enough folic acid. Folic acid is essential in the development of cells. It is also needed for the nervous system to function properly. Without adequate folic acid, the fetus's neural tube, brain, spine, and nerves are likely to develop abnormally.

The average person needs about two hundred micrograms (0.2 milligrams) of folic acid each day. A pregnant woman needs double this amount. And, because the neural tube and brain start forming in the first month of pregnancy, before a woman knows she is pregnant, the U.S. Public Health Service recommends that all women of childbearing age take a folic acid supplement. Then even if a pregnancy is unplanned, the fetus is protected from neural tube defects.

# Multivitamins Help

To help ensure that the fetus develops normally, it is important that expectant mothers increase their daily intake of nutrients vital to fetal growth. Because pregnant women need larger than normal amounts of some nutrients, this cannot always be accomplished through diet alone. That is why pregnant women are often prescribed a prenatal vitamin supplement.

These multivitamins are specially formulated for pregnant women. They contain just the right amount of every vitamin needed for optimal fetal development. For example, they contain enough vitamin A to boost cell growth, but not enough to cause birth defects.

Prenatal vitamins also contain a number of essential minerals including iron. Lack of iron leads to abnormal fetal brain development, miscarriages, and stillbirths. The body uses iron to manufacture red blood cells that carry food and oxygen to every cell in the body. Without ample red blood cells, the fetus does not receive enough oxygen or nutrition. That is why pregnant women require thirty milligrams of iron, double the amount that other people need. Eating foods that are rich in iron, like red meat and spinach, and taking prenatal vitamins with iron help ensure that the fetus gets enough oxygen and nutrients to develop and grow properly.

Because folic acid is so crucial in preventing neural tube defects, in 1998 the U.S. Food and Drug Administration required that it be added to all grain and cereal products. Some of the foods that are enriched with folic acid include breads, cereal, flour, pasta, and rice. However, for a pregnant woman to get enough folic acid through enriched food alone, she would have to eat four servings of cereal or a whole loaf of bread each day. But even a slight increase in folic acid consumption reduces birth defects. A 2004 study by the Centers for Disease Control found that before the folic acid food enrichment requirement went into effect, about four thousand babies a year were born with neural tube defects. After the requirement took effect, this number dropped to about three thousand babies.

Ellen Chase, the first runner-up in the 2000 Mrs. America Pageant, is the mother of a daughter with spina bifida. During her pregnancy she did not take a supplement with folic acid. After her daughter's birth, she learned about the importance of folic acid and took supplements. She attributes the health of her two younger children to the supplements. Chase explains: "It is important for all women of child-bearing age to take folic acid. Girls should begin taking it as soon as they begin menstruating. It's too late to take it after you find out you're pregnant, because the neural tube is formed in the first three weeks of pregnancy."[51]

## Avoiding Dangerous Activities

Avoiding dangerous activities and exposure to dangerous substances is another way to prevent many birth defects. To prevent learning disabilities and mental retardation, all illegal drugs should be avoided. So too should prescribed medications and over-the-counter drugs unless they are taken under a doctor's care and supervision.

Cigarette smoke, whether first- or secondhand, is also avoided. Inhaling smoke and nicotine, a chemical in cigarettes, reduces the amount of oxygen in the mother's blood and therefore the amount of oxygen the fetus receives. Nicotine increases the fetus's heart rate and interferes with the mother's and fetus's ability to absorb vitamins like vitamin C and folic acid. Smoking is clearly linked to premature births, low birth weight, and craniosynostosis, a birth defect in which the baby's skull forms incorrectly, resulting in an abnormally shaped head. According to the Centers for Disease Control, developing fetuses that are exposed to five to fourteen cigarettes per day are four times as likely to be born with craniosynostosis as those not exposed to maternal smoking.

Smoking may also be connected to learning disabilities and heart, lung, and neural tube defects. Experts at KidsHealth, a Web site dedicated to the health of children, warn expectant mothers:

> Would you light a cigarette, put it in your baby's mouth, and encourage the child to puff away? As ridiculous as this question seems, pregnant women who continue to smoke are allowing their fetus to smoke too. The smoking mother passes nicotine and oxygen-poor blood to the growing baby. The risks of smoking to the fetus include stillbirths, birth defects, low birth weight, sudden infant death syndrome and cancer.[52]

## Radiation and Herbicides

Exposure to radiation and herbicides should also be shunned. Radiation from X-rays can destroy or damage developing fetal cells by causing them to mutate. That is why dentists and doctors always ask patients if there is any chance they might be pregnant before X-rays are administered.

*Radiation from dental X-rays can cause fetal cells to mutate.*

# Cosmic Radiation

In an effort to see if exposure to cosmic radiation leads to birth defects, scientists are studying its effects on pregnant women who fly frequently. Cosmic radiation is similar to that produced by a nuclear blast. It consists of charged particles that come from the sun and deep space and bombard Earth. When these particles reach Earth's atmosphere they are absorbed before they reach the ground. Consequently, there is significantly more cosmic radiation at flying altitudes than at sea level. Therefore, women who fly on a daily basis, such as flight attendants, air marshals, and pilots, are exposed to more cosmic radiation than other people.

Scientists do not know whether cosmic radiation is as harmful to fetal development as other forms of radiation, or if frequent flyers are exposed to high enough quantities of it to be damaging. In order to find out, a number of studies are being conducted.

In the meantime, the Federal Aviation Administration (FAA) considers airline crew members to be occupationally exposed to radiation, and the Occupational Safety and Health Administration provides guidelines on cosmic radiation exposure limits.

In an effort to help flight crew members minimize their contact with cosmic radiation, the FAA offers a computer program that allows individuals to calculate cosmic radiation levels for various air flights based on the flying altitude and duration. The FAA suggests that pregnant crew members use these calculations in planning their flight schedules in order to limit their exposure. For example, pregnant crew members are advised to switch from international to national or regional flights, which are shorter and fly at lower altitudes.

Herbicides, too, are harmful, especially when pregnant women work with herbicides or live in close proximity to fields that are treated with them. A 2003 study by the Environmental Protection Agency analyzed 43,634 births in rural communities in Montana, Minnesota, North Dakota, and South Dakota. The study compared the prevalence of birth defects in babies born in counties where the herbicide chlorophenoxyl is and is not used. The study found a 50 percent greater incidence of birth defects in the counties with the highest usage of chlorophenoxyl. The risk appears to be greatest when the mothers are exposed during the third to eighth week of pregnancy. To protect their babies, expectant mothers who work with herbicides often take a leave of absence from their jobs. Women who live near fields treated with herbicides can lessen their risk by planning their pregnancy so that the first two months occur during the times of the year when the fields are not treated.

Avoiding contact with cat feces is another way a woman can prevent birth defects. Toxoplasma, a parasite that infected cats shed in their feces, can spread to people who handle infected feces. It can be transmitted to humans when they handle cat feces in cat litter or infected soil. If a pregnant woman becomes infected with toxoplasma there is a 40 percent chance of the fetus becoming infected. Approximately one in one thousand babies in the United States is born infected with toxoplasma each year. This can cause impaired vision, mental retardation, hearing loss, cerebral palsy, and learning disabilities in the baby. By not handling cat litter during pregnancy and wearing protective gloves when she works in the garden, a pregnant woman can avoid the damage the toxoplasma can do. Lexington, Kentucky, obstetrician David Hager says: "I give everyone the same advice: stay away from cat litter . . . and you shouldn't be at risk."[53]

It is true that there is no way to guarantee that every baby is strong and healthy. However, by taking steps to ensure a healthy pregnancy many birth defects can be prevented. Peter Nathanielsz, the director of Cornell University's Laboratory for Pregnancy, tells pregnant women: "The health and nutritional state of your body—the baby's home—is the single most important factor in the baby's growth."[54]

# Chapter 5

# What the Future Holds

SCIENTISTS HAVE NOT yet identified all the causes of birth defects. In an effort to prevent birth defects, researchers are focusing their studies on pinpointing unknown causes of birth defects. Once these have been identified, steps can be taken to keep pregnant women from being exposed to them. In addition, scientists are developing new treatments that can cure many birth defects.

## Phthalates

Scientists are looking at the link between birth defects and exposure to potentially hazardous substances called phthalates. A phthalate is a chemical softener that is used in plastics, solvents, vinyl building products such as flooring, roof film, and wall coverings, as well as in medical supplies, toys, detergents, and personal care products like nail polish, shampoo, fragrances, hair spray, deodorants, and cosmetics. Phthalates can enter a person's body through the mouth, skin, or lungs. Once the chemicals enter a pregnant woman's bloodstream, they pass to the fetus through the placenta.

A number of laboratory studies have looked at the effect of phthalates on fetal mice. In 2000 the U.S. Environmental Protection Agency conducted one such study in Research Triangle Park, North Carolina, on ninety pregnant mice. The mice were divided into seven groups. One group acted as a control. The other six groups were each administered a different phthalate in their food from the fourteenth day of their pregnancy until three days after the birth of their babies. The offspring were then examined for birth defects at birth through puberty. The researchers found that exposure to phthalates damaged the developing reproductive organs in male, but not female, fetuses and caused fertility problems once the male mice reached puberty. Depending on the phthalate that the mother was administered, as many as 87 percent of the male offspring had malformed testicles and penises compared to 0 percent of the control group. Other animal studies reported similar results.

These same phthalates are used in many products humans come in contact with on a daily basis. Scientists do not yet know if exposure to phthalates has the same effect on developing humans as it does on animals, but many researchers think it is likely. In 2001 scientists from the Centers for Disease Control in Atlanta

*A series of recent experiments involving fetal mice (pictured) has identified a possible link between hazardous chemicals called phthalates and birth defects.*

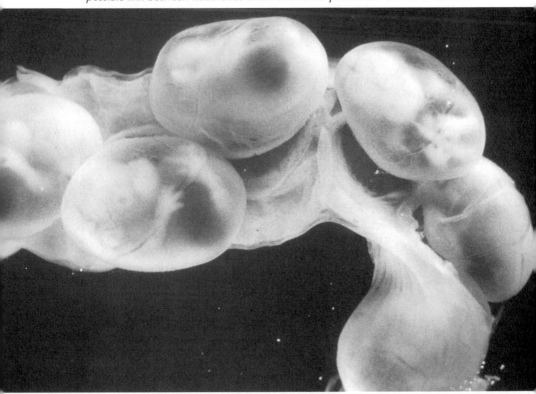

tested urine samples from people throughout the United States for phthalates. The scientists say that if phthalates are found in a person's urine, the chemicals are also present in the person's bloodstream since they cannot all be eliminated.

The scientists were surprised at how high the phthalate levels were. The highest concentrations were found in women between the ages of twenty and forty. This group's phthalate levels were nearly 50 percent higher than the rest of the population. This is particularly troubling because this group is most likely to become pregnant.

Scientists are currently working on studies that compare the levels of phthalates found in the humans with the levels that were found to cause birth defects in mice. Many, like National Academy of Science phthalate expert Louis J. Guillette Jr., theorize that the levels will prove to be similar. Guillette says: "If you take the (CDC's human) exposure data, that these things are occurring at high concentrations, and you look at the experimental data on the developing rats [mice], you realize that the doses aren't that far apart."[55]

---

*Experts advise pregnant women to avoid exposure to products that have high concentrations of phthalates, such as nail polish.*

If it is proven that phthalates do cause human birth defects, the government may ban the use of the chemicals. In the meantime many experts are advising pregnant women to avoid exposure to phthalates, and many personal care products manufacturers are producing new products without phthalates. Susannah, who is five months pregnant, stopped using all personal care products that contain phthalates after learning about the possible danger they pose to her baby. She says: "It's a lifestyle change. I used to buy anything. Now I look at all the labels. My feeling is if I can make these purchasing changes, then it is better for me and my child."[56]

## Refined Carbohydrates and Birth Defects

Scientists at the University of California at Berkeley are taking another approach. They know that foods contaminated with mercury and foodborne pathogens cause birth defects. They are investigating if exposure to other foods can also damage fetal development. In particular, they are examining whether eating a diet high in refined carbohydrates plays a role in causing birth defects. Refined carbohydrates are commonly found in foods like cookies, candy, cake, sodas, fruit punch, white bread, and sweetened breakfast cereals.

The consumption of refined carbohydrates causes the body to release large amounts of glucose (a sugar) into the bloodstream. Excess glucose depletes the body's production of inositol, a chemical messenger that is involved in the manufacturing of cells. Scientists theorize that when excess glucose is passed to the fetus it decreases fetal cell production, causing the cells to form abnormally or not form at all.

In fact, scientists already know that pregnant women with diabetes, a disease characterized by high levels of blood sugar, are more prone to have problems during pregnancy and give birth to premature babies. More troubling, a number of animal studies have identified higher than normal levels of neural tube defects in the offspring of test animals fed a diet high in refined carbohydrates.

Based on these findings, in 2003 Berkeley scientists compared the prepregnancy and pregnancy diets of almost one thousand mothers with and without children with neural tube defects. The

*Pregnant women should choose foods wisely. Sweets and pastries result in elevated blood sugar levels, which have been linked to birth defects.*

scientists found that the subjects who had consumed the most refined carbohydrates were twice as likely as the other subjects to have a baby with neural tube defects.

Because of this study, obstetricians, along with experts at the March of Dimes, are making an effort to raise awareness of the link between a sugary diet and neural tube defects. In the process, they are advising women of childbearing age to limit their consumption of refined carbohydrates before and during pregnancy. These changes, they think, will help reduce the number of babies born with neural tube defects. The mother of a child with spina bifida comments:

> If these foods are a significant factor, then women need to be made aware of this research. I wouldn't wish what happened to me on anyone. It was awful. We found out I was carrying a child with spina bifida in a scan at about twenty-two weeks [of pregnancy]. I took folic acid in the two months before I got pregnant and I made sure I ate a lot of fruit and salads but . . . I had eaten quite a bit of sugar. Who doesn't eat cereals? We need more research.[57]

Indeed, more studies are currently under way. If the link between high blood sugar levels and neural tube defects is proven, then a diet low in refined carbohydrates is likely to be prescribed for pregnant women.

## Gene Therapy

While some scientists are trying to identify unknown causes of birth defects, other scientists are using a process known as gene therapy to prevent, cure, and treat birth defects. Gene therapy involves replacing or modifying defective genes with normal genes. By replacing or altering mutant genes in individuals with inherited diseases, scientists say they can treat and cure existing conditions like cystic fibrosis and hemophilia. And, if mutant genes can be replaced in an embryo, then scientists can change the embryo's gene pool, making it possible to stop transmission of the mutant genes to future generations.

Modifying embryonic genes is still in its early stages. But scientists have already replaced defective genes after birth. To do this, scientists insert a healthy gene into a virus that has been modified in a laboratory to render it less harmful. This is done because genes cannot travel through the bloodstream on their own. They must be carried by something that can move easily through the body. Viruses move freely through the bloodstream. Once viruses reach their target they deliver their genes directly to a person's cells. Because such viruses have been modified, they most often, but not always, do not make individuals ill.

Employing this method, in 1998 researchers in the Children's Hospital of Philadelphia used gene therapy to treat dogs with hemophilia. To do this, the scientists inserted a healthy gene into a modified common cold virus. The healthy gene produces a blood-clotting factor absent in people and animals with hemophilia. The virus was then injected into the dogs' leg muscles. The scientists theorized that the virus would stimulate leg muscle cells to produce the clotting factor, which would then be released into the dogs' bloodstreams. Just as the scientists predicted, the dogs' blood clotting improved significantly. Before the treatment it took more than an hour for the dogs' blood to clot, compared to normal blood-clotting time of about six minutes. After the treatment, this time dropped to fifteen minutes and, after a year, the gene was still working.

A similar 1999 study at Stanford University, Palo Alto, California, reported like results. Because of the success of these studies, clinical trials on humans have begun. In fact, a 2003 human study at Royal Prince Alfred Hospital in Sydney, Australia, on two men with hemophilia produced a significant increase in the subjects' blood-clotting factor for more than a month. Says John Rusko, head of gene therapy at Royal Prince Albert Hospital, "The results are exciting and a step towards curing hemophilia with one injection."[58]

## Delivering Genes Without a Virus

Scientists are also using gene therapy to treat cystic fibrosis. Individuals with cystic fibrosis lack a gene that produces a protein that balances the levels of salt and water in the nose and lungs. Without this protein, a thick sticky substance forms in airways of people with cystic fibrosis, making it difficult for them to breathe. Scientists have already re-created the gene needed to produce the protein. However, because individuals with cystic fibrosis have weak respiratory systems and often suffer from chronic respiratory infections, even a modified cold virus can cause serious problems for these individuals. To combat this problem, scientist at Copernicus Therapeutics, a biotechnology company in Cleveland, Ohio, have created a way to deliver a healthy gene into a person's airways without the use of a virus. This can be done because the airways are readily accessible. Therefore, if a gene can be made small enough it can be carried by inhaled air directly to cells that line the airways.

The scientists created a way to condense strands of DNA, the substance that genes are composed of. The DNA is compacted into tiny nanoparticles that can be sprayed into a person's nostrils. In the nose, the DNA mixes with air that is inhaled and goes directly into the nasal passageway.

In 2003 researchers at the Case Western Reserve University School of Medicine and the University Hospitals of Cleveland, Ohio, and Children's Hospital in Denver, Colorado, tested this gene therapy delivery method on twelve adults with cystic fibrosis. The subjects were given the healthy gene via a saline solution that was dripped into their nasal passages. The researchers monitored salt levels in the subjects' nasal tissues before and after the gene was administered. They also took samples of nasal tissue,

*Forced to live his first months of life in a plastic enclosure because of a serious genetic disease, this boy underwent experimental gene therapy and now lives a normal life.*

*In this 1992 photo, a researcher experiments with a nasal spray of genetically engineered proteins to help cystic fibrosis patients to breathe more easily.*

which were examined for the presence of the corrective protein. The protein was present in eight of the subjects. Scientists say that the presence of the protein indicates that the delivery system works. Now that scientists know that the delivery system is effective, future studies will examine the effect of the therapy on cystic fibrosis symptoms. Scientists are optimistic that in the future the therapy may be an effective way to eliminate respiratory problems that plague individuals with cystic fibrosis. Cystic Fibrosis Foundation president Robert J. Beall explains: "This gene therapy research has exciting potential as a new approach to addressing the genetic root cause of CF [cystic fibrosis]. . . . We eagerly anticipate results of future clinical studies utilizing this novel approach."[59]

## Gene Therapy That Builds Muscles

In addition to hemophilia and cystic fibrosis, scientists are currently conducting gene therapy research on more than 250 other diseases. Among these are PKU, sickle-cell anemia, fragile X syndrome, and muscular dystrophy.

Researchers at the University of Washington in Seattle successfully used gene therapy to treat muscular dystrophy in mice. Individuals with muscular dystrophy cannot produce dystrophin, a protein that keeps muscles from breaking down. Without dystrophin, their muscles waste away. In 2002 Washington scientists successfully inserted a gene that stimulates dystrophin production in laboratory mice with muscular dystrophy. The gene worked so well that it not only stopped muscle wasting in the mice, it also reversed existing damage. Researcher Jeffery S. Chamberlain explains: "We expect to build on these results in the continuing search for a way to treat a horrible disease. Our results indicate that gene therapy could be used not only to halt or prevent this disease, but also to restore normal muscle function. . . . These results are extremely encouraging."[60]

In 2004 scientists at the Centre Hospitality de Universidad Quebec, Canada, built on the Washington study in a human trial in which three brothers with muscular dystrophy were treated using a similar method. These scientists took cells from the boys' father containing genes that stimulate the production of dystrophin and transplanted them into the boys' shin muscles. As the scientists expected, the boys started to produce dystrophin, which stimulated new muscle growth. However, unlike in the mice, previous muscle damage was not reversed. Scientists do not know why this is so. To learn more, larger studies are planned for the future. George Henderson, spokesperson for Muscular Dystrophy Canada, explains: "This research really is a very strong indicator of a direction we will pursue aggressively and can lead to treatment. . . . It's a very important first step along a long path. It will be some time before we see it translated into bedside care or treatment for Duchenne muscular dystrophy."[61]

Scientists do not know how long it will take before gene therapy will be commonly used. But experts at Special Child, a Web site dedicated to birth defect research, predict: "Gene therapy could redefine the practice of medicine in the next century. The very concept of altering one's genetic makeup when drug treatment

# A New Discovery That Helps Babies with Heart Defects

*For many babies with heart defects, a heart transplant is their only chance for survival. Unfortunately, because of the limited quantities of hearts available and the fact that the transplanted heart must be the correct size and blood type, many babies die before a heart is found.*

*An article on the* CBS News *Web site explains how cardiologist Lori West of the Hospital for Sick Children in Toronto is helping more babies survive:*

"In late 1995, there was an infant waiting and we were offered a heart, and then the blood type was wrong," says West. "And turning down the organ . . . it became clear to me . . . that we needed to go back and really examine this whole issue."

The child died, and that reminded West of some experiments she had done six years before. In transplanting organs into mice, she noticed something strange about infant mice. It turned out that baby mice were able to tolerate organs that weren't an exact match.

is not an option is phenomenal. Gene therapy is expected to one day cure 4,000 known genetic disorders. . . . Gene therapy is on track to be the most powerful curative and diagnostic tool ever."[62]

## Stem Cell Research

Other scientists are working on transplanting stem cells into defective organs of people with birth defects. Stem cells are human cells that are capable of changing into and repairing any cell in the body.

Most stem cells are harvested from human embryos created at in vitro fertilization clinics but never implanted, and from

West suspected their immune systems were just so immature that they didn't recognize the mismatched organs as foreign tissue.

Shortly thereafter a baby named Caleb Schroeder was born at the Hospital for Sick Children with a defective heart. Without a new heart, Caleb was not expected to live and the only heart available was the wrong blood type. West convinced Caleb's parents and the hospital ethics committee to let her transplant the mismatched heart into Caleb. She theorized that like the mice, at one month old, Caleb's immune system was not developed enough to reject the heart.

The surgery proved to be a success. In fact, today Caleb is a healthy young boy. Like any transplant patient, Caleb must take antirejection drugs, but otherwise he is living a normal life.

The surgery provided another unexpected benefit. Caleb's immune system now accepts any blood type. This means that if the need ever arises, he can receive a blood transfusion from any blood type, not just his own type O blood.

As a result of the success of Caleb's surgery, about thirty-eight similar surgeries have been performed throughout the world.

aborted fetuses. However, due to ethical issues, there are governmental limits on the use of embryos and aborted fetuses for this purpose. To ease the shortage of embryonic stem cells, some stem cells are taken from the bone marrow of adults and children. Once the cells are harvested, they are taken to a laboratory where scientists have developed a method to make the cells multiply. The original and newly formed stem cells are cultured and kept in petri dishes where they can survive indefinitely.

Researchers theorize that healthy stem cells can be inserted into individuals with a wide variety of birth defects. If their theory is correct, the transplanted cells will quickly take on the characteristics of the organ they are transplanted into. Then, the cells will take over for defective cells, correcting the problem and essentially curing the birth defect.

To test the effectiveness of stem cells in healing inherited diseases, in 1999 Harvard scientists injected neural stem cells into the brains of mice that had been infected with Tay-Sachs disease. Individuals with the disease do not produce a chemical that is essential in protecting the health of the nervous system. Without it, cells in the nervous system break down and die.

The mice were unable to produce the chemical. However, once the stem cells were implanted the mice began producing the missing chemical, thereby correcting the root cause of the disease. As a result of this study, a number of human trials are being conducted. In fact, doctors at Duke University in North Carolina have already done six stem cell transplants in children with Tay-Sachs disease. In every case the transplant stopped the progress of the disease. The scientists used neural stem cells because Tay-Sachs is a disease of the nervous system, and earlier studies proved that neural stem cells easily give rise to healthy nerve cells.

Other human trials are investigating the effectiveness of stem cells in healing sickle-cell anemia. In 1998 a twelve-year-old boy with the disease was given bone marrow stem cells intravenously at Egelston Children's Hospital in Atlanta. The stem cells passed through the boy's bloodstream and found their way to his bone marrow where red blood cells are produced. The healthy stem cells took over for the boy's defective cells, producing normal red blood cells rather than the sticky sickle cells that characterize the disease. Since the transplant the boy has been free of sickle-cell anemia. However, he must take antirejection drugs.

A number of other successful stem cell transplants on sickle-cell patients have also been reported. Sixty-nine such transplants have been reported in St. Louis Hospital, Paris, France, with an 85 percent disease-free survival rate.

Despite the success rates, stem cell transplants are still in the experimental stage. But scientists expect the process to become more common in the future. Talking about the potential that stem cell transplants have in treating sickle-cell anemia, Ronald Hoffman, the president of the American Society of Hematology, says: "It's going to change the way we treat individuals with this disorder. If they're truly cured . . . they're going to be freed of the consequence of a chronic disease."[63]

## Transplanting Stem Cells in Fetuses

Experiments are also ongoing on stem cell transplants for muscular dystrophy, fragile X syndrome, thalassemia, cerebral palsy, and other birth defects. Some are even attempting to transplant stem cells to fetuses, thus curing the birth defect before the baby is born. In fact, forty-two stem cell transplants have been performed on fetuses in the United States with varying results. One successful 1996 case at the Children's Hospital in Philadelphia cured a fetus with a fatal birth defect that affects the immune

*Mattie Stepanek (left), a poet who touched millions of people, died of muscular dystrophy at the age of thirteen. Fortunately, radical new treatments may save others with birth defects.*

system and makes it impossible for individuals to fight infections. Babies with the disorder rarely live more than a year. In this case bone marrow stem cells harvested from the fetus's father were injected through the mother's abdomen into the twelve-week-old fetus. Bone marrow stem cells develop into red and white blood cells, and a variety of immune cells. Doctors predicted that the transplanted stem cells would quickly multiply and replace the damaged immune cells in the fetus.

They were right. At birth the baby showed no signs of the immune disorder and after eleven months appears to be normal and healthy. Scientists say that prebirth bone marrow stem cell transplants should cure fetuses with sickle-cell anemia and thalassemia in the same way, and studies are ongoing. Alan W. Flake, the doctor who performed the transplant, explains: "If this strategy can be made to work . . . there are broad implications for treating human disease. This approach could potentially target any diseases that are now treatable with bone marrow transplants. These include blood diseases such as leukemia, thalassemia, and sickle cell disease as well as many inherited immunodeficiency disorders."[64]

Currently, Dr. Flake is working on transplanting stem cells into fetuses with muscular dystrophy. So far, laboratory experiments have shown that stem cells transplanted into fetal mice with muscular dystrophy develop into healthy muscle cells. Human trials are likely to take place soon.

Indeed, with the development of gene and stem cell therapies and the identification of previously unknown causes of birth defects, someday soon the fight against birth defects may be won. Says New Jersey birth defect researcher Ira Black: "I think we have every reason to be optimistic."[65]

# Notes

## Introduction: A Common Problem

1. Quoted in Charlotte Tallman, "March of Dimes Targets Premature Birth," *Las Cruces Sun News*, November 25, 2003, p. 5A.
2. Quoted in Tallman, "March of Dimes Targets Premature Birth."
3. Quoted in Experience Journal, "About Katie." www.experience journal.com/cardiac/sharing/aboutkatie.shtm4.
4. Quoted in Charlotte Tallman, "Education Seen as Key to Reducing Birth Defects," *Las Cruces Sun News*, March 2, 2004, p. 5A.
5. March of Dimes, "In Support of the SMART Mom Act." www.modimes.org/aboutus/855_1947.asp.
6. Quoted in Allan F. Platt and Alan Sacerdote, *Hope and Destiny*. Roscoe, IL: Hilton, 2002, pp. 154–156.

## Chapter 1: What Are Birth Defects?

7. Quoted in Platt and Sacerdote, *Hope and Destiny*, p. 131.
8. American Heart Association, "Heart to Heart," September 20, 2003. www.americanheart.org/presenter.jhtml?identifier=3015263.
9. Quoted in Platt and Sacerdote, *Hope and Destiny*, p. 30.
10. Quoted in Special Child, "Fragile X Syndrome," Disorder Zone Archives. www.specialchild.com/archives/dz-008.html.
11. Quoted in Tom Sullivan, *Special Parent, Special Child*. New York: Putnam, 1995, p. 199.
12. Quoted in Special Child, "Fetal Alcohol Syndrome," Disorder Zone Archives. www.specialchild.com/archives/dz-011.html.
13. Center for Drug Evaluation and Research, "Medication Guide Accutane Capsules." www.fda.gov/cder/drug/infopage/accu tane/medicationguide.htm.

14. Bonnie, personal interview by author, Las Cruces, New Mexico, September 10, 2004.

15. Quoted in Associated Press, "Birth Defects Linked to Obesity," *CBSNews.com*, May 5, 2003. www.cbsnews.com/stories/2003/04/08/health/main548286.shtml.

### Chapter 2: Diagnosing and Treating Birth Defects

16. Mitchell Zuckoff, *Choosing Naia*. Boston: Beacon, 2002, p. 16.

17. Cindy, personal interview by author, Las Cruces, New Mexico, August 14, 2004.

18. Bonnie, interview.

19. Quoted in Special Child, "Spina Bifida," Disorder Zone Archives. www.specialchild.com/archives/dz-005.html.

20. Holly Manzanera, Compassionate Care Midwifery Services. www.midwifesa.com/services.htm.

21. Quoted in Amy E. Tracy and Dianne I. Maroney, *Your Premature Baby and Child*. New York: Berkley, 1999, p. 102.

22. Quoted in Special Child, "Fragile X Syndrome."

23. Quoted in Zane's Lane, "Zane Alexander Gardner." http://members.iserv.net/lynetteg/zaneFS.htm.

24. Jeremy Gerking, "The Rae Ellen Gerking Story," Fetal Treatment Center, University of California San Francisco. www.fetalsurgery.ucsf.edu/gerking.htm.

25. Quoted in Tracy and Maroney, *"Your Premature Baby and Child*, p. 112.

26. Quoted in Charlotte Tallman, "Child Gets a Second Chance at Life," *Las Cruces Sun News*, March 17, 2003, p. 1A.

27. Quoted in Hospital for Sick Children, "Meet Daniel: Daniel's Letter." www.sickkids.on.ca/Foundation/custom/pom_daniel.asp?s=Patients+Features+%2D+M.

### Chapter 3: Living with Birth Defects

28. Marie A. Kennedy, *My Perfect Son Has Cerebral Palsy*. Bloomington, IN: First Books Library, 2001, p. 29.

29. Kennedy, *My Perfect Son Has Cerebral Palsy*, p. 43.

30. Quoted in Cerebral Palsy Connection, "My Story and Cerebral Palsy 1." www.cpconnection.com/LivingCP/My_Story1.htm.

31. Quoted in Margaret Wahl, "Physical Therapy—Flexibility, Fitness and Fun," *Quest*, June 2000. www.mdausa.org/publications/Quest/q73therapy.html.

32. Quoted in Tracy and Maroney, *Your Premature Baby and Child*, p. 130.

33. Lisa C. Downs-Gleeson, "The Job That Nobody Wanted?" Special Child. www.specialchild.com/archives/ia-047.html.

34. Quoted in Cochlear War, "Myth and Facts." www.cochlearwar.com/myths_and_facts.html.

35. Quoted in Tara Wood, "Talking with Technology," *Quest*, March/April 2003. www.mdausa.org/publications/Quest/q102technology.cfm.

36. Quoted in Margaret Wahl, "Taking to the Water," *Quest*, June 2000. www.mdausa.org/publications/Quest/q73therapy3.html.

37. Quoted in Wahl, "Taking to the Water."

38. Quoted in Carol Sowell, "School Days Learning New Ways to Learn," *Quest*, August 1998. www.mdausa.org/publications/Quest/q54school.html.

39. Quoted in Sowell, "School Days Learning New Ways to Learn."

40. Quoted in Sowell, "School Days Learning New Ways to Learn."

41. Downs-Gleeson, "The Job That Nobody Wanted?"

42. Quoted in Victoria Potter, "Summer Camp for Children with Heart Disease," Medscape. www.medscape.com/viewarticle/408306_3.

43. Quoted in Special Child, "Spina Bifida."

## Chapter 4: Preventing Birth Defects

44. David, telephone interview by author, San Francisco, California, August 30, 2004.

45. Bonnie, interview.

46. Quoted in Platt and Sacerdote, *Hope and Destiny*, p. 30.

47. Quoted in Platt and Sacerdote, *Hope and Destiny*, p. 30.

48. Quoted in Epinions.com, "The Search for a Vaccine—The Importance of Pre-Conception Check-Ups," October 2, 2003. www. epinions.com/content_3558449284.

49. Michael L. Schultz, "Getting Ready for a Healthy Pregnancy," Texas Medical Association, Medem Network. www.mlschultz. yourmd.com/ypol/userMain.asp?siteid=17124.

50. Quoted in Maureen Connolly, "Foods to Avoid During Pregnancy," Your Baby Today. www.yourbabytoday.com/baby place/pregnancy/preg_health/food.

51. Quoted in Virginia Society for Healthcare Marketing and Public Relations, "A Little 'Pill' Can Make a Big Difference." www.vshmpr.com/modbfolic.pdf.

52. KidsHealth, "Staying Healthy During Pregnancy." http:// kidshealth.org/parent/pregnancy_newborn/pregnancy/preg _health_p2.html.

53. Quoted in Melissa Ramsdell, "Kitty Litter and Pregnancy," Your Baby Today. www.yourbabytoday.com/babyplace/preg nancy/preg_health_kitty.

54. Peter Nathanielsz, *The Prenatal Prescription*. New York: Harper-Collins, 2001, p. 44.

**Chapter 5: What the Future Holds**

55. Quoted in Daniel P. Jones, "CDC Eyes Chemicals' Level in Humans," *Indianapolis Star*, August 26, 2000. www.indystar.com.

56. Quoted in Sally Jacobs, "Scent of Trouble Surrounds Cosmetics," *Boston Globe*, October 16, 2002. www.boston.com.

57. Quoted in Earth Crash Earth Spirit, "*London Telegraph* Article," November 23, 2003. www.eces.org/articles/000484.php.

58. Quoted in Dwayne Hunter, "One-Shot Therapy Cure for Hemophilia Nearer," *Better Humans*, May 13, 2003. www.better humans.com/News/news.aspx?:articleID=2003-05-13-1.

59. Quoted in EurekAlert! "Cystic Fibrosis Gene Therapy Trial Results Encouraging," April 29, 2003. www.eurekalert.org/ pub_releases/2003-04/uhoc-cfg042803.php.

60. Quoted in EurekAlert! "Gene Therapy Reverses Muscular Dystrophy in Animal Model," September 16, 2002. www.eurek alert.org/pub_releases/2002-09/uow-gtr091302.php.

61. Quoted in Karen Palmer, "Gene Therapy Promising for Muscular Dystrophy," *Toronto Star*, February 19, 2004. www.thestar. com.

62. Special Child, "Information Avenue Archives, Gene Therapy." www.specialchild.com/archives/ia-027.html.

63. Quoted in Associated Press, "French Researchers Say Stem Cell Transplants Successful in Sickle Cell Patients," Inteli-Health, December 9, 2002. www.intelihealth.com/IH/ihtIH/ WSIHW000/333/7228/358861.html.

64. Quoted in EurekAlert! "Prenatal Stem Cell Transplants May Open the Door to Organ Transplants, Treating Genetic Diseases," November 6, 2002. www.eurekalert.org/pub_releases /2002-11/chop-pse110602.php.

65. Quoted in Bob Groves, "Creation of Neurons at New Brunswick, N.J. Medical School Advances Research," *The Record*, May 12, 2004. http://web11.epnet.com/citation.asp?tb=1&_ug=sid +6639F30C%2DB150%2D46EA%2DB5.

# *Glossary*

**amniocentesis:** A test in which fluid is taken from inside the womb and analyzed for chromosomal and genetic abnormalities.

**amniotic fluid:** The fluid that surrounds the fetus in the womb.

**birth defect:** An abnormality of the structure or function of the body that develops in a fetus during pregnancy.

**chromosome:** A capsulelike structure that contains genes.

**DNA (deoxyribonucleic acid):** The substance that genes are composed of.

**dominant gene:** A gene that carries traits that are always inherited.

**embryo:** An unborn baby under eight weeks old.

**fetus:** An unborn baby more than eight weeks old.

**folic acid:** One of the B vitamins, folic acid is essential for normal fetal growth. Lack of the vitamin is linked to neural tube defects.

**functional birth defects:** Birth defects that affect the way the body functions.

**gene:** A heredity unit that directs the body how to develop and gives each individual his or her unique characteristics.

**infectious agents:** Germs that cause infection such as bacteria, fungi, and viruses.

**in vitro fertilization:** A process in which an egg taken from a woman is fertilized in a laboratory with sperm taken from a male. The embryo is then implanted into the female's womb.

**isolette:** A heated crib enclosed in clear plastic that provides a sick newborn infant in the NICU with a warm, quiet environment.

**multifactorial birth defects:** Birth defects that are caused by a number of different factors.

**neonatal intensive care unit (NICU):** A special section of the hospital dedicated to the care of sick newborns.

**neural tube:** The part of the body that connects the spine to the nervous system.

**obstetrician:** A doctor who specializes in the care of pregnant women.

**pediatrician:** A doctor who specializes in the care of infants and children.

**phthalate:** A chemical found in plastics and personal care products that has been linked to birth defects.

**placenta:** A tubelike structure through which the fetus receives vital substances necessary for life, like nutrients and oxygen.

**premature birth:** Birth that occurs before the thirty-seventh week of pregnancy.

**prenatal:** Before birth.

**stillbirth:** A birth in which the baby is dead upon delivery.

**structural birth defects:** Birth defects that affect the formation or structure of the body.

**triple-marker test:** A blood test given to pregnant women that detects a number of developing birth defects in the fetus.

**ultrasound:** An imaging technique that uses sound waves to create an image of the fetus.

# *Organizations to Contact*

### American Heart Association

7272 Greenville Ave. Dallas, TX 75231
(800) 242-8721
www.americanheart.org

Offers educational material and support groups for every type of heart disease including problems caused by birth defects.

### American Sickle Cell Association

10300 Carnegie Ave. Cleveland, OH 44106
(216) 229-8600
www.ascaa.org

Provides information and support for people with sickle-cell anemia.

### Association of Birth Defect Research for Children

930 Woodcock Rd. Orlando, FL 32803
(407) 895-0802
www.birthdefects.org

Offers fact sheets on many different birth defects and provides a support network for parents of babies with birth defects to connect them with other parents who face the same issues.

### Cystic Fibrosis Foundation

6931 Arlington Rd. Bethesda, MD 20814-5231
(800) FIGHT-CF
www.cff.org

Provides information about cystic fibrosis and sponsors research into the disease.

## March of Dimes

1275 Mamaroneck Ave. White Plains, NY 10605
(914) 428-7100
www.modimes.org

One of the largest organizations working to end birth defects. With chapters throughout the United States the March of Dimes sponsors research and offers information on different birth defects, birth defect prevention, and pregnancy issues.

## Muscular Dystrophy Association

3300 E. Sunrise Dr. Tucson, AZ 85718
(800) 572-1717
www.mdausa.org

Provides information about muscular dystrophy; sponsors research, summer camps, and support groups; and connects patients with doctors.

## National Easter Seals Society

230 W. Monroe St. Chicago, IL 60606-4802
(800) 221-6827
www.easter-seals.org

Provides information, rehabilitation, support services, and help in obtaining assistive devices for people with cerebral palsy and other disabilities.

# For Further Reading

## Books

Susan Dudley Gold, *Cystic Fibrosis*. Berkeley Heights, NJ: Enslow, 2000. A simple book that looks at the cause, diagnosis, treatment, and challenges of cystic fibrosis.

Lisa Iannucci, *Birth Defects*. Berkeley Heights, NJ: Enslow, 2000. A young adult book that discusses the causes, diagnosis, and treatment of birth defects.

Jeanne Warren Lindsay and Jean Brunelli, *Your Pregnancy and Newborn Journey*. Buena Park, CA: Morning Glory, 1999. An easy book that talks about pregnancy, fetal development, and steps to take to prevent birth defects.

Alvin Silverstein, Virginia Silverstein, and Laura Silverstein Nunn, *Sickle Cell Anemia*. Springfield, NJ: Enslow, 1997. A young adult book that covers the causes, diagnosis, and treatment of sickle-cell anemia.

Sherry Bennet Warhauer, *Everyday Heroes: Extraordinary Dogs Among Us*. New York: Howell, 1998. Stories and pictures of heroic service dogs, some of which serve individuals with birth defects.

## Web Sites

**CDC: National Center on Birth Defects and Developmental Disabilities** (www.cdc.gov/ncbddd). The Centers for Disease Control offers information about birth defect prevention.

**Children's Hospital Boston** (www.childrenshospital.org). The hospital provides information on fetal surgery and the neonatal intensive care unit.

**Hospital for Sick Kids** (www.sickkids.on.ca). University of Toronto Hospital for Sick Kids is one of the largest pediatric hospitals in the world. The Web site offers treatment information about numerous birth defects, talks about research, and has success stories.

**KidsHealth** (www.kidshealth.org). Dedicated to children's health, KidsHealth provides information on different diseases and health issues.

**Special Child** (www.specialchild.com). This site offers a newsletter, information, success stories, and a large disorder zone with facts about many birth defects.

**Your Baby Today** (yourbabytoday.com). This sites gives advice on what to do to ensure a healthy pregnancy.

# Works Consulted

## Books

Marie A. Kennedy, *My Perfect Son Has Cerebral Palsy*. Bloomington, IN: First Books Library, 2001. The mother of a son with cerebral palsy talks about the challenges her son faces and how the family copes.

Judith Kleinfeld, Barbara Morse, and Siobhan Wescott, *Fantastic Antone Grows Up*. Fairbanks: University of Alaska Press, 2000. Case studies of young people with fetal alcohol syndrome, describing what living with fetal alcohol syndrome is like.

Peter Nathanielsz, *The Prenatal Prescription*. New York: Harper-Collins, 2001. Talks about the steps pregnant women should take to ensure a healthy pregnancy and baby. It focuses on the role of nutrition.

Allan F. Platt and Alan Sacerdote, *Hope and Destiny*. Roscoe, IL: Hilton, 2002. A clear guide to sickle-cell anemia.

Tom Sullivan, *Special Parent, Special Child*. New York: Putnam, 1995. Each chapter is an interview with a different family dealing with a different birth defect.

Amy E. Tracy and Dianne I. Maroney, *Your Premature Baby and Child*. New York: Berkley, 1999. Although not focused specifically on birth defects, this book provides information about premature babies, medical concerns, and caring for babies with special needs.

Mitchell Zuckoff, *Choosing Naia*. Boston: Beacon, 2002. Parents of a child with Down syndrome and heart defects tell their story.

## Periodicals

Associated Press, "Disease Testing For Newborn Babies Varies," *Las Cruces Sun News*, September 14, 2004.

Coralee Carlson, "Transplant Baby Doing Well," *Albuquerque Journal*, March 20, 2004.

Michelle Kaufman, "Making Waves," *Albuquerque Journal*, June 21, 2004.

Charlotte Tallman, "Child Gets a Second Chance at Life," *Las Cruces Sun News*, March 17, 2003.

Charlotte Tallman, "Education Seen as Key to Reducing Birth Defects," *Las Cruces Sun News*, March 2, 2004.

Charlotte Tallman. "March of Dimes Targets Premature Birth," *Las Cruces Sun News*, November 25, 2003.


## Internet Sources

American Heart Association, "Heart to Heart," September 20, 2003. www.americanheart.org/presenter.jhtml?identifier=3015263.

Apgar.net, "Virginia Apgar Pictures, Articles, and Information." www.apgar.net/virginia.

Associated Press, "Birth Defects Linked to Obesity," *CBSNews.com*, May 5, 2003. www.cbsnews.com/stories/2003/04/08/health/main 548286.shtml.

*CBS News.com*, "Change of Heart." www.cbsnews.com/stories/ 2004/03/29/60minutes/main609225.shtml.

Center for Drug Evaluation and Research, "Medication Guide Accutane Capsules." www.fda.gov/cder/drug/infopage/accu tane/medicationguide.htm.

Cerebral Palsy Connection, "My Story and Cerebral Palsy 1." www.cpconnection.com/LivingCP/My_Story1.htm.

Cochlear War, "Myth and Facts." www.cochlearwar.com/myths _and_facts.html.

Maureen Connolly, "Foods to Avoid During Pregnancy," Your Baby Today. www.yourbabytoday.com/babyplace/pregnancy/ preg_health/food.

Lisa C. Downs-Gleeson, "The Job That Nobody Wanted?" Special Child. www.specialchild.com/archives/ia-047.html.

Earth Crash Earth Spirit, "*London Telegraph* Article," November 23, 2003. www.eces.org/articles/000484.php.

Epinions.com, "The Search for a Vaccine—The Importance of Pre-Conception Check-Ups," October 2, 2003. www.epinions. com/content_3558449284.

EurekAlert! "Cystic Fibrosis Gene Therapy Trial Results Encouraging," April 29, 2003. www.eurekalert.org/pub_releases/2003-04/uhoc-cfg042803.php.

———, "Gene Therapy Reverses Muscular Dystrophy in Animal Model," September 16, 2002. www.eurekalert.org/pub_releases/2002-09/uow-gtr091302.php.

———, "Prenatal Stem Cell Transplants May Open the Door to Organ Transplants, Treating Genetic Diseases," November 6, 2002. www.eurekalert.org/pub_releases/2002-11/chop-pse110602. php.

Experience Journal, "About Katie." www.experiencejournal.com/cardiac/sharing/aboutkatie.shtm4.

Jeremy Gerking, "The Rae Ellen Gerking Story," Fetal Treatment Center, University of California San Francisco. www.fetalsurgery.ucsf.edu/gerking.htm.

Bob Groves, "Creation of Neurons at New Brunswick, N.J. Medical School Advances Research," *The Record*, May 12, 2004. http://web11.epnet.com/citation.asp?tb=1&_ug=sid+6639F30C%2DB150%2D46EA%2 DB5.

Hospital for Sick Children, "Meet Daniel: Daniel's Letter." www.sickkids.on.ca/Foundation/custom/pom_daniel.asp?s=Patients+Features+%2D+M.

Dwayne Hunter, "One-Shot Therapy Cure for Hemophilia Nearer," *Better Humans*, May 13, 2003. www.betterhumans.com/News/news.aspx?articleID=2003-05-13-1.

InteliHealth, "French Researchers Say Stem Cell Transplants Successful in Sickle Cell Patients," InteliHealth, December 9, 2002. www.intelihealth.com/IH/ihtIH/WSIHW000/333/7228/358861.html.

Sally Jacobs, "Scent of Trouble Surrounds Cosmetics," *Boston Globe*, October 16, 2002. www.boston.com.

Daniel P. Jones, "CDC Eyes Chemicals' Level in Humans," *Indianapolis Star*, August 26, 2000. www.indystar.com.

KidsHealth, "Staying Healthy During Pregnancy." http://kids health.org/parent/pregnancy_newborn/pregnancy/preg_ health_p2.html.

Holly Manzanera, Compassionate Care Midwifery Services. www. midwifesa.com/services.htm.

March of Dimes, "Folic Acid." www.modimes.org/pnhec/887.asp.

———, "In Support of the SMART Mom Act." www.modimes.org/ aboutus/855_1947.asp.

Karen Palmer, "Gene Therapy Promising for Muscular Dystrophy," *Toronto Star*, February 19, 2004. www.thestar.com.

Personal MD, "Miscarriage Risk Slightly Higher in Flights Attendants." www.personalmd.com/news/a1999062106.shtml.

Victoria Potter, "Summer Camp for Children with Heart Disease," Medscape. www.medscape.com/viewarticle/408306_3.

Melissa Ramsdell, "Kitty Litter and Pregnancy," Your Baby Today. www.yourbabytoday.com/babyplace/pregnancy/preg_ health_kitty.

Michael L. Schultz, "Getting Ready for a Healthy Pregnancy," Texas Medical Association, Medem Network. www.mlschultz. yourmd.com/ypol/userMain.asp?siteid=17124.

Carol Sowell, "School Days Learning New Ways to Learn," *Quest*, August 1998. www.mdausa.org/publications/Quest/q54school. html.

Special Child, "Assistance Dogs—More Than Just Man's Best Friend." www.specialchild.com/archives/ia-009.html.

———, "Fetal Alcohol Syndrome," Disorder Zone Archives. www. specialchild.com/archives/dz-011.html.

———, "Fragile X Syndrome," Disorder Zone Archives. www. specialchild.com/archives/dz-008.html.

————, "Information Avenue Archives, Gene Therapy." www. specialchild.com/archives/ia-027.html.

————, "Spina Bifida," Disorder Zone Archives. www.specialchild. com/archives/dz-005.html.

Virginia Society for Healthcare Marketing and Public Relations, "A Little 'Pill' Can Make a Big Difference." www.vshmpr.com/ modbfolic.pdf.

Margaret Wahl, "Physical Therapy—Flexibility, Fitness and Fun," *Quest*, June 2000. www.mdausa.org/publications/Quest/q73 therapy.html.

————, "Taking to the Water," *Quest*, June 2000. www.mdausaorg/ publications/Quest/q73therapy3.html.

Tara Wood, "Talking with Technology," *Quest*, March/April 2003. www.mdausa.org/publications/Quest/q102technology.cfm.

Zane's Lane, "Zane Alexander Gardner." http://members.iserv.net /lynetteg/zaneFS.htm.

# Index

# Picture Credits

Cover photo: AP Wide World Photos
AP/Wide World Photos, 7, 8–9, 20, 36, 45, 51, 59, 83, 84, 89
© Lester V. Bergman/CORBIS, 12
© Cameron/CORBIS, 80
Centers for Disease Control, 21
© Dan Habib/The Concord Monitor/CORBIS, 44
© Julie Houck/CORBIS, 67
© Christos Kalohoridis/CORBIS, 73
© Michael Keller/CORBIS, 65
Brandy Noon, 15, 17, 35
© Tom Nebbia/CORBIS, 46
© Richard T. Nowitz/CORBIS, 31, 57
© Gabe Palmer/CORBIS, 18
Photos.com, 26, 62, 69, 78
© Roger Ressmeyer/CORBIS, 53
Kon Sasaki/Photo Researchers, Inc., 77
Akhtar Soomro/EPA/Landov, 41
Saturn Stills/Photo Researchers, Inc., 29
© Bill Varie/CORBIS, 61
Hattie Young/Photo Researchers, Inc., 48

## About the Author

Barbara Sheen has been a writer and educator for more than thirty years. She writes in English and Spanish. Her writing has been published in the United States and Europe. She lives in New Mexico with her family, where she enjoys swimming, walking, reading, gardening, and cooking.